Dreamy
Filthy
Suicide

Brian j. Kamerer

This is a work of fiction. Any references to real people, events, establishments, organizations or locales are intended only to give the fiction a sense of reality and authenticity. Other names, characters and incidents are either the product of the author's imagination or are used fictitiously.

WRONGMAN PRESS

Columbus, OH 43202

www.wrongmanproductions.com

Copyright 2006 by Brian Kamerer

Cover designed by Brian Kamerer and Lehr Beidleschies

Printed in the USA.

This book is dedicated to everyone who hasn't killed him or herself, and to anyone who has.

THE FIRST PART

Dreaming had always made Darren Fishy's life sad-complicated. Because he would sleep-walk all puppet like, no control over his actions. Once, when he was nine years old, heavily under the influence of such a dream, Darren killed his sleeping Dad with an axe. Darren was wearing nothing but tighty whities and socks that night (he had not yet made the switch from tighty whities to boxer shorts).

He climbed from his bed and walked downstairs to the garage, where he retrieved the axe that his Dad had used earlier that day to chop firewood. He then marched up the stairs into his Dad's room and struck him several times. One might wonder why his Dad hadn't woken up after that first swing, screaming agony-ouch and maybe attempting to disarm his son, as most fathers would do in such a situation. This was made near-impossible for Darren's father, however, because of the fact that Darren had buried the axe deeply into his Dad's forehead, which smart-doctors say probably killed him. It was all over in one juicy-sickening thunk. The rest of the blows were simply the dreamy overkill of a sleepwalking, axe-wielding nine year old, and served only to create a wholly unnecessary mess of blood and skull fragments. Some days it rains twice. Darren then wet himself while standing over his father's mangled corpse, all gross.

+

The orphanage Darren lived in when he was nine years old was run by an old-strange lady. She overran every square inch of the place with cats. And the cats begat/fucked more cats and Darren wasn't very happy there. Not that the cats *themselves* bothered him. In fact, he considered some of them to be his closest friends. He liked the kittens more than the full grown cats, as most people do, but he made sure to give his attention to them all. He was kind of a dork about it.

Instead, the problem was that most of the orphans

didn't appreciate the cats so much. This often caused Darren to not so much like the kids. Every time a group of boys hurt some of the cats by throwing them, or putting them in a homemade flying machine and *then* throwing them, Darren cried inside for the little kitties. Especially the baby kittens. But he never said anything to try and stop the vicious-mean kids. Because Darren couldn't talk.

That's not exactly true. He could talk. But he *didn't* very often, kind of because he was traumatized and kind of because he forgot to. For example, sometimes people would say hello to him and he would raise his head up, open his eyes wide, and then turn back around, simply forgetting that one is supposed to call out a response before one continues watching television. Darren liked to watch <u>Saved by the Bell</u>. This was a show about popular kids in a high school. He could watch almost four episodes a day. And he did.

+

He claimed to have been dreaming that he was, "killing a cow." This dream struck judges as a disturbing dream for a nine year old (or anyone for that matter) to have, but they didn't want to convict the boy just for having creepy-uneasy dreams. So since he had a history of night terrors and showed plenty of remorse for his actions (he cried, all red-eyed, through several hearings with judges and psychologists and his lawyer, Bob) he was not convicted of any crime/bad-thing. But he had become an orphan. A sort of famous orphan with a lethal sleep walking problem.

+

This was kind of the scenario when Darren met a boy named Jessie at the orphanage.

"Hey kid."

Darren's eyebrows rose, still looking at the TV.

"Ms. Bitch said to clean the table off."

Jessie was not calling the lady in charge of the orphanage a bitch in an insulting kind of way. Her name, in fact, was Ms. Bitchington. She told the kids earlier on, "Just call me Ms. Bitch. I know you'll start saying it behind my back anyway, so you might as well say it to my face." But not all of the kids did. Darren felt weird saying it to her face. Because Ms. Bitch wasn't really a bitch, she wasn't mean to any of the kids. In fact, she barely even talked to anyone at all, giving her attention to only a select *few* of the kids. A better name for her would have been Ms. Selectively Attentive to the Orphan Children.

When Darren made no attempt to get up and clean off the table, Jessie remarked, "That's just what she said." Darren still didn't look up from his TV show. "I know about your Dad," Jessie threw in as almost an afterthought. When he saw that Darren was not going to react, he walked away.

+

When Darren was about thirteen, he and Jessie attended a private school together. Around this time, some of the younger kids in school found out about Darren's Dad. This made Darren extremely popular with hard knocked eleven and twelve-year-olds, who maybe dreamed of killing a Dad or step-Dad themselves. They'd point and follow-stalk him all day long at school, a rag-tag group trailing behind the oblivious Darren throughout the school day.

Jessie wanted Darren to use this fame to start a cult like gang of younger gothy punky thuggy grungy kids. Actually, that's not true, *Jessie* wanted to start the gang *himself*, using Darren's fame. They were eating synthetic tacos for dinner at a fast food restaurant when he asked if Darren minded.

"So, do you care?"

"I wouldn't have to do much?"

"No, I would do everything, you would be like the king or queen or whatever."

"Why do you want a gang?"

"To sell drugs and enforce and shit."

Jessie was straight faced.

Darren had trouble sometimes knowing the difference between Jessie's joking voice and serious voice. But after staring at Jessie for a second he decided to just say, "Ok." And they ate their remaining tacos. They were delicious.

+

A little blue pill is what Darren took before sleep time. Right after he brushed his teeth. This was so he could fall into a deep-peaceful, blank-dreamless, not-hurt-anyone kind of sleep. After that first murder with his dad, a big old judge told Darren, "From now on, you sleep only, and I mean *only* under lock and key."

But Darren's lawyer Bob found a doctor who found the little blue pill that allowed Darren to not sleep in a jail-cell-bedroom and not sleepwalk around at night, killing loved ones. Darren was one of those unheard of kinds of people with no money and a really good lawyer.

+

Darren stared down at his hands as the guy talk-babbled. He had already washed them by this point, but their was still dry blood-speckle on his arms, above his wrist. He was picking at it, in a police station. Nine years old. He had a big police coat on and not much else. Just socks and an uncomfortable pair of tighty whities, (his underwear was soaked through in blood, but he kept them on (he turned down the fresh pair the police offered him because he was afraid they would make him change in front of a bunch of strangers)).

"...and I am telling you Son, the nerve...I mean the downright irrefutable fucking nerve of these sons of bitches, putting you through this! FUCK! I swear to God, Son. You will be rich after the lawsuits we are going to throw their way, know and understand that we are talking about five or even six, I repeat, six figures here..."

Darren wasn't really listening to the guy in the suit and the trench coat talking to him. He was still in a hand-picking daze and the man seemed to be talking to himself anyway.

"What do you say, Darren?"

Darren woke up at the mention of his name. He raised his eyebrows, but didn't look at the man.

"Well, how about it, Darren?"

"I don't think I know?"

There was a police officer in the corner of the room and he yelled, "Next!" Then the guy in the suit had to leave, saying, "Oh, for Christ's sake," under his breath on the way out. And another guy in a suit came into the room to join Darren and the cop.

This had been happening all day. Darren's case became famous real quick. Lawyers were lined up out the door, offering their services for free. This was a case/client that promised notoriety. And so all these lawyers came in and talked very fast to Darren about things he didn't understand, and then they said something like:

"You with me sport?"

"It's just me and you now buddy."

"You're gonna need me now, pal."

To Darren it sounded like he was supposed to pick a new Dad. And he didn't want to. He'd only just then lost his old one.

+

Darren's Dad was kind of a drunk. Not drunk in the abusive and mean sense of the word. More like the pained widower sense. Darren didn't mind the drinking though, because often when his Dad drank glass after glass of whiskey with ice in it, he would do nothing but talk to Darren. He told him all kinds of stories about his wife and the army. Well, not really all kinds. Mostly just stories about those two subjects. But it felt like all kinds of stories to Darren, because stories about his Mom and his Dad's army days were really all Darren ever wanted to hear about.

+

The thirteenth man in a suit, trying to be Darren's attorney came into the room and said, "Hi, I'm Bob."

Darren just stared at him. After a couple of seconds of silence, both Darren and Bob exchanging stares, Darren said, "I'm tired."

"I bet. Where are you sleeping tonight?"

The kid shrugged and so Bob looked to the cop who pointed towards a black couch up against the wall.

"Do you have any blankets?" Bob asked the cop. The cop told Bob where he might be able to find blankets and so he left to retrieve them.   While he was gone, the cop who had remained so quiet standing in the corner all day, said to Darren, "Bob is a pretty good guy.   And I've seen plenty of lawyers around here." When Bob came back into the room, he made up a bed for Darren on the couch, with folded up blankets as a pillow. Then he tucked Darren in and asked, "You want anything?" Darren said that he wanted TV.

"What shows do you like?"

"And I want my Dad."

"I know, buddy."

Darren started crying.

"I want my Dad more than TV."

Bob's voice was calm.

"I know you do."

Bob placed a hand on Darren's shoulder and after a few minutes, his tears died down from sadness to sleepiness and Darren told Bob, "I watch <u>Saved by the Bell</u>, mostly."

"I don't know that one."

"It's pretty cool."

"Cool."

Darren closed his eyes.

"Bob?"

"Yeah."

"Could you be my lawyer?"

"Sure Darren."

+

I woke up wet and sticky and at first I thought I went to
the bathroom in bed, but there was a different smell. I saw
that I had an axe in my hand and that I was in my Dad's bed
and covered in blood and for a second, my dream came back to
me, the cow and the axe and there was some kind of General
or something, but I'm frozen solid, can't move in this huge
puddle of blood and I'm thinking that I'm frozen cause I'm
dying, but I am actually just paralyzed-scared from all the
blood and so I tried to wake up my Dad cause I thought I was
hurt and dying and bleeding to death. And it took a lot of
concentration just to roll over and look at him cause I was *that*
scared (like my body was still asleep) and his face was torn and
bloody and empty and eyes open rolled back. And I still
couldn't move and I really wanted to but I was shock-trapped
underneath the white soaked-red sheets. I laid there and
remembered being right outside a huge green field in my
dream, and being handed the axe. The General told me,
"Nobody likes this part. Not supposed to. But you gotta do it.
So *we* know you can." And I saw there was light blue sky
floating on top of the green field just out of my reach and I
knew I was close and didn't have a choice anymore cause the
General himself was watching me, and then lots of soldiers
were watching me and I then I was in my underwear,
completely embarrassed in front of all these people, and I knew
what I had to do to get out of this, so I pulled back the axe and
closed my eyes and I heard and hated the ka-chunck sound
but I pulled back and hit again and again and again and
probably more, then I dropped the axe and walked out towards
the field and I felt the relief sink in and I sunk down deep into
the soft grass. Happy, just staring up at the sky knowing that

I had finally completed my training and I would become what my father had always wanted me to be. A navy seal. I couldn't wait to tell him the good news, and I woke up with a bit of this anticipation still in me and there I was, all tucked into Dad's bed, covered in blood.

+

Darren layed on the couch watching TV at his new foster parent's house. This was a good time of the day, because he was able to sneak in an hour of <u>Saved by the Bell</u> reruns. His new parents would be described as hippies to people described as *not* hippies. And they wouldn't let Darren watch most TV. They *hated* <u>Saved by the Bell</u>. So, Darren could only watch the reruns from four to five, when nobody else was home. Darren's father said the show was, "A poor message, wrapped in commercials." Darren thought the show was funny.

"You've already seen this fucking episode."

Darren flinched, he hadn't realized that Jessie had let himself in the house.

"I mean, *I've* seen this episode and I don't even watch the goddamn show. Now, let's go. We have a meeting."

"After this." Darren spoke with his face mashed up against a pillow.

"How much longer?"

"Till five."

"Fine."

Darren heard a flicking noise and the sound of Jessie sucking. Jessie offered him the joint but Darren said, "No thanks." The boys were in the living room.

"That's probably a good idea." Jessie inhaled deeply, "It's dusted."

Darren didn't know what *dusted* meant.

"O.K."

"With PCP."

Darren wasn't sure what that meant either.

"O.K."

"And coke."

"Aight."

Darren and Jessie listened to rap music, and Darren occasionally liked to try and speak in a similar style. Sometimes he said aight, pronounced Ah-ight (ight as in sight) instead of saying alright.

Darren's Hippie-Dad, who was home early from work, walked into the room and upon seeing the boys, promptly had a fit. "Darren, what did I tell you, man! I do not want this fascist television program watched or even playing inside my house!"

Darren didn't say he was sorry.

"What do you have to say for yourself?"

"Well, I didn't smoke the pot?"

Hippie-Dad looked down and saw that Jessie was indeed smoking a joint right next to him. Jessie nodded to the Hippie-Dad, and the Hippie-Dad looked back to Darren and asked, "Why not?" Darren shrugged and looked towards his show and said, "I guess, because, it's dusted." Hippie-Dad turned back to Jessie, all shocked, "How old are you, man?" Jessie just shrugged, all glazy-confused by the question. He was twelve.

+

Darren listened to rap music, pretty much just because Jessie did. He wasn't sure how Jessie had heard about all this cool/beautiful music. Because the only radio station that played new music in his town, only played rock music. Although, occasionally/not very often, they would play a rap song. But still only rap songs that featured white rappers, like the Beastie Boys and later on in life, Eminem. Darren wondered why they didn't play music by the black rappers that him and Jessie liked. After all, these guys were just as good and usually better than the white ones. Jessie told Darren this was because the radio station or at least the majority of their listeners were racists. Darren wondered if all of these people even knew they were racists? They must have found out though, because eventually this radio station changed names and turned into a station that only played black rappers.

+

When Darren was thirteen, he lived in a house with a rich-successful young couple. He liked it there because they had the information super highway. On this World Wide Web, Darren was able to look at pictures of naked, sex-people. From there he found a place called a chat room, some of these chat rooms were specifically designed as places where people could go and type incredibly dirty/exciting words and sentences to strangers who were presumably home at their computers. Some of these people did this a lot. Darren became one of them.

He learned that some people are dark, intricate, in depth, and specific about sex. He learned about things like rape role play, spanking, hard bondage, anal sex, fisting, bestiality, pedophilia, deep-throat-gagging, gangbanging, and urination-defecation fetishes.

Sometimes if Darren could find someone bland enough, who just liked to type out regular kinds of sex acts, he would talk to them as a means to try and masturbate. However, the first time he did this, he was not sure what a male human was supposed to type to a female human, so as to make her feel good and comfortable-sexy. However, he did think he had a good idea of what he wanted a girl to type to him. So, Darren joined the chatroom and pretended to be a girl, deciding it to be an easier way to get the sentences he wanted to see typed, typed.

For the most part though, Darren liked to talk to people to see how much deep-dark stuff they would tell him. He was interested in what people let loose, within the safety-pillow of anonymity. Sometimes the things that people typed to Darren made him wonder about the whole entire world. "What's going on in everybody's heads?"

+

Before the first meeting of Jessie's gang, Darren and Jessie had breakfast for dinner. Jessie said, "This is going to be amazing."

"I don't have to do anything, right?"

"No, you're fine. Do you watch that mafia show, The Sopranos?"

Darren was eating pancakes and Jessie was drinking coffee.

"No. Hippie-Dad said that he read it was racist towards Italians, like Olive Garden commercials."

"Well, its not. They even have conversations about that kind of thing on the show. About how Italians aren't all mobsters, but like, how they are just the *best* mobsters."

"Oh."

Jessie grabbed something in his pants and started pooring it into his coffee. Darren saw that it was cough syrup.

"I like that show and all that Godfather mafia stuff, but I'm pretty sure that this gang should be more like an old school rap gang."

"Dig."

Darren was trying to say, "dig," more often now, ever since Jessie made him watch the movie, *The Warriors,* in order to research the proper way to lead a gang. In *The Warriors,* one of the characters says, "Can you dig it?" really loud to a bunch of gangs and all the gangs cheer to suggest that they can, in fact, dig it. But Darren was just trying to say, "dig," more often. Because, whereas he thought he could pull off, "dig," he wasn't sure he could get away with, "Can you dig it?" Darren did find that a lot of rappers thought they could get away with saying, "Can you dig it?" In the rap music they listened to, the phrase, "Can you dig it?" was often either spoken or sampled. It was a theme.

What made Darren fall for Jessie, in that strictly friendly kind of way, was the fact that Jessie talked to him. The other kids in the orphanage were too scared to talk to him. They were afraid of being killed by Darren, being ostracized by the rest of the kids for associating with the weird kid, or just afraid that if they talked to him, they might have to talk about the murder of his Dad, as if Darren would just bring it up, like it was something he enjoyed chatting about. Jessie did not share this fear with the kids, in fact he talked about the Dad-murder very often with Darren.   "It's just weird. I mean, why did you walk up stairs to your Dad's room, if you didn't walk up any stairs in your dream?"

"I don't know."

Darren was lovingly petting a kitten who he had secretly-privately named Sneakers. Sneakers was purring contentedly and pushing her little orange head against Darren, wanting more and more head scratching/love. And Darren was happy to give it. The kitties were the only kind of physical affection he had in his life. Some other names he gave to the cats were, Laboratory, Spades and Screech.

"It's like someone was controlling you like a video game or something."

Darren shrugged and Jessie narrowed his eyes toward Darren's.

"You're sure you're not lying bout all this dream stuff?"

Darren shook his head like to silently say, yes.

"Cause you could tell me."

Darren shrugged.

At Darren's wealthy, big-clean house, when his yuppie-parents were out partying (they went out a lot of nights to have a good time, and Darren enjoyed them leaving) he sat down at the computer and entered the world wide info web. He entered into a singles chat room as Prettybaby10. In the chatroom he asked if anyone wanted to talk on IM to a hot young girl (Darren liked to talk privately, to people, because they would say stranger- weirder things in exclusive *instant message* conversations, even more so than in the public chat rooms) . This is how he met the only sort of girlfriend he would ever have.

Prettybaby10: A/s/L ?

Sammyman: 30, Male, and I am not going to tell you where I am from. You?

Prettybaby10: i am a 14 year old girl and i hav blond hair and i live in california

Sammyman: I bet you do.

Prettybaby10: i wanna take my shirt off and put ur penis in my mouth and give u a blowjob

Sammyman: Don't you feel *silly*?

Darren paused and thought about this question.

Prettybaby10: i thought this is what u wanted.

Prettybaby10:   i asked if u wanted to cyber?

Sammyman: I'm not even a guy. I lied. I just wanted to see what people said.

Darren grew slightly aroused.

Prettybaby10: if u r a girl, it is ok we could keep talkin

Sammyman: I told you, I don't want to cyber.

Prettybaby10: NO, i didn't mean like lesbian cybering

Sammyman: I just think that if you like sex so much, why don't you go out and try to find another person to have sex with? What *you* like isn't sex, what *you* like is typing about sex to a screen.

Prettybaby10: im a guy!

Sammyman: I figured.

Then she signed off of the Information Web Highway and Darren saved the name, Sammyman, onto his buddy list.

Darren and Jessie rode on a white moped to the first meeting of their gang. Jessie had found a warehouse that seemed to be at least temporarily abandoned. Jessie drove since it was *his* moped, with Darren on the back, and while he moved the throttle with one hand, he chugged down the rest of the bottle of red/thick, Dr. Pepper-ish tasting cough syrup and then tossed it to the ground with the other.

They arrived and Jessie lit a joint and Darren saw that their was only about six kids waiting outside the warehouse. They all seemed younger, between the ages of nine and eleven. One of the kids had a mohawk and a skateboard. Well, not the kind of mohawk that is shaved on the sides, but the kind where the hair is the same length all over, then styled and hair-sprayed up to the sky, in the middle. This kind of mohawk is not considered to be as punk rock as the kind that is shaved on the sides. Two of the kids had trench coats and eye make up on and little upside down crosses painted on their cheek and forehead. One of the kids was dressed in an old flannel shirt and ripped blue jeans complete with a very cool chain attached to his wallet. At least, *Darren* thought the chain looked cool. There were also two kids who were wearing really-really baggy sweat suits with big hoods and the suits looked really-really soft and comfy like pillow-clothes. There was only one other kid. He was dressed very uninterestingly. Jessie got things going.

"This way."

The warehouse looked bigger on the inside and Darren was not surprised to see that Jessie had already been there. The office type room that Jessie was leading the kids into had a couple of couches and a stereo and the kids sat down. Darren didn't go inside though, because next to the room, just outside, he saw that there was a fold out lawn chair pointed towards a little TV. Jessie saw him looking at the TV. "Just for you, man." Then Jessie shut the door as Darren flipped on <u>Saved by the Bell</u> and sat down.

"Aight. Welcome to our first meeting."

All the kids looked around at each other, unsure how to act. One of the thuggy kids asked what the fuck the name of the gang was, and one of the gothy kids asked when they would get to meet Darren.

"There is no name of this gang."

The kids wondered why. Jessie dragged on his joint, and then with a puffed-out chest he said, "SO, you guys don't have a name to talk shit about and brag about and (he exhaled) make everything more famous than it should be." The kids nodded.

The young boy who was dressed uninterestingly raised his hand and then stumbled, "Um...what about Darren?"

"You will meet Darren when you are ready. First things first. Initiation time."

The kids sized each other up, unsure of what they would be asked to do.

"You all get high, right?"

Everyone kind of nodded and the thuggy kids giggled.

"Aight, there are seven corncob pipes and seven lighters underneath that table. Everyone take one, but don't hit it yet."

Everyone grabbed a pipe. The grungy kid asked, "What are we gonna have to do, man?" And a thuggy kid, eyeing the gothy kids, said, "Yeah, I'm not doing gay stuff man. No way."

"We are just getting high together. As a gang. And then you're in."

The punky kid said, "My kind of gang." And the thuggy kids laughed, "Shit, we're already blazed mothafuck!"

"Ok, three, two, one. "

Jessie hit his joint and watched as everyone lit their lighters and inhaled deeply.

"Ok, now hold it in as long as you can."

Jessie talked very quickly.

"What you just inhaled is a powerful extract made from the hallucinogenic plant Salvia Divenorum. It is designed to be twenty times more powerful than the plant in it's natural state. Good luck!"

Jessie turned the lights to pitch black and hit the stereo. Ears-hurting, pounding, screechy, electronic music poured from it. What was happening in the minds of those kids was all stormy/mystery. Some were probably trying to fight the trip, all full strength-intensity in a matter of seconds. Some were probably yelling for help, although no one would be able to hear over the noise-music. Some were probably trying to figure out where or even *what* they were. And as Jessie had planned, most *everybody* was experiencing a different kind of scared.

Jessie immediately slipped out the door. He saw that Darren was still sitting there. He was watching the Saved by the Bell episode where a character, quasi-addicted to caffeine pills, is freaking out in front of another character. Jessie said to the screen, "stupid bitch," and then grabbed Darren and yanked him into the dark. Jessie handed Darren some kind of stick, and pushed him ontop of the table in the center. Darren thought he heard screaming, but wasn't sure if it was part of the horrible music or if the kids were in some kind of pain. Then Jessie turned a red strobe light on Darren, illuminating him in a seizure-flash red spotlight. In between blinks, he squinted and saw that he was holding an ax and that the kids were writhing below him and seemed retarded-horrified. Darren also got scared. Then over the music, propelled by a bullhorn, Jessie's voice boomed.

"I AM DARREN FISHY! I SLAUGHTERED MY OWN FATHER IN MY SLEEP WITH THIS FUCKING AX! NO MAN WILL TELL ME WHAT TO DO! I HAVE MURDERED WITH EASE DEEP IN MY FUCKING DREAMS! AND NOW THAT I AM AWAKE, I WILL TEAR THROUGH THE FLESH OF ANYONE OR THING THAT GETS IN MY WAY! SO YOU HAD BETTER FUCKING BE WITH ME! CAUSE OTHERWISE I AM FUCKING AGAINST YOU!"

Jessie flicked the red strobe off and then switched the track on the stereo so as to make a nice cozy-mellow song start playing. Then he pushed Darren out of the room, flipped a little night-light on and told the kids to relax and that they would all feel fine in a couple of minutes. "We are happy to have you as part of the team." Then he shut the door and him and Darren left the warehouse.

It only took ten minutes for the effects of the

hallucinogen to fade and when it did, the kids turned the light back on and found an envelope taped to the door. Inside was a hand written letter and seven joints. The letter read:

You have all been reborn. You work for Darren now and he will look out for you always. There should be complimentary welcome-joints for each of you (don't worry, it's just regular happy-pot). We will meet here again tomorrow, at the same time.

Yours truly,

Jessie

Darren's

Assistant

+

Hippie-Dad always got Darren up early for school. Together they would sit and eat breakfast, sometimes with Hippie-Mom, depending on whether she worked morning or night. But rain or shine the dad was there serving not eggs, not bacon and not milk, but hashbrowns, and pancakes with no butter and lots of maple syrup. Because it was O.K. to bleed maple trees, but not O.K. to use the bodily products of animals. This made sense to Darren. Because animals were like people, but not quite as technologically capable as people, so animals were like retarded people and you wouldn't even think about eating a retarded person, would you?

The Hippie-Dad would complain to Darren about some woman who should be allowed to die if she wants to kill herself or have a lesbian partner kill her in a mercy sort of way or something like that. All the complaints would get jumbled up in Darren's head.

The Hippie-Dad thought that gay people should be allowed to marry each other, being that they are also just human beings like you and I, but the Hippie-Dad *also* didn't think that marriage was really relevant/interesting these days, even though he himself was married. Darren didn't often pay attention, because it was hard work. Not to say that Darren disagreed. He just didn't think that he would ever know what all was right for the world. So, why pay attention?

But Darren liked the fact that his Hippie-Dad always had an answer for his questions (although, he didn't have very many questions). One thing Darren *did* ask was, "What happens when we die?"

This was one of the few subjects that concerned Darren. After all, he had two dead parents to worry about. When he popped the question during breakfast; his Hippie-Dad told him with no hesitation, "Well man, a lot of people will feed you a bunch of strange stories about Heaven and Hell and a Devil with a pitch fork and pointy tail, but see that's just designed by society to try and keep you in line. See, they try to scare you into thinking that you have to follow their rules or else you'll burn, but I'm telling you this now man, it's all just a bunch of hocus pocus fairy tale stuff, what really happens is you start again."

Darren stopped eating in order to listen closely. Hippie-Dad spoke fast, so it was hard for him to pay attention, but Darren didn't want to miss a word.

"Yup, it's called reincarnation. See, the spirit, I mean like, the essence of man, it travels into another vessel in the physical world. And like it tries to correct the mistakes of it's past lives. Do you understand?"

Darren said, "Dig," which really-really encouraged Hippie-Dad to continue.

"The thing is though, that we lose all of our memories and once again, we have to guide ourselves using only our feelings, but in truth its like the world that is guiding us."

Darren was starting to not understand, but he still nodded, because he didn't want to seem all dumb.

"Once our spirits finally find enlightenment in the physical world, they are able to rest in like, a euphoric state, which is called Nirvana."

Darren had heard of Nirvana.

"And see this is different than like heaven or whatever, because it comes through *enlightenment*..."

Darren thought Nirvana was a band.

"...praying is like, supposed to accomplish the same things as meditation, but you're just kidding yourself..."

Darren thought that maybe Nirvana had gotten their band name from the Nirvana-place Hippie-Dad was talking about.

"...self deception man, it's just self deception..."

Darren liked the Nirvana video where they broke/thrashed everything in school.

+

The last conversation that Darren had with Jessie at the orphanage, was in a coat closet. When Darren came home from lunch with Bob and put his coat away, Jessie scared him really close to death by grabbing Darren and pulling him in. He didn't have to cover Darren's mouth because Darren didn't scream. Darren had never even so much as yelled before. It wasn't in his nature to be loud. Jessie didn't turn the light on. They talked in the dark.

"I am fucking out of here."

Darren was still jarble-shook from the scare, but he recognized Jessie's voice.

"Um."

"Fuck her man. That fucking bitch. (In this case Jessie *was* referring to Ms. Bitch as a bitch in an insulting kind of way, like to insinuate that she was not a human woman, but actually a female dog) She wants my fucking nuts man."

Darren didn't say anything because he wasn't exactly sure what Jessie had meant.

"I'm serious man, she wants my fucking nuts."

"What does that *mean*?" Darren spoke into a big fluffy coat.

"It means that she fucking wants to fuck me, asshole!"

Darren didn't say anything. He was shocked like with static electricity. He didn't know anything at all about fucking. But he didn't think that old women or little boys did it. Let alone with each other.

"But how do you know that she *wants your nuts*?"

"She found out that I was selling cigarettes and crack at school cause somebody here told her, or she found my stash or something, so in her room she tells me she's gonna send me to jail and picks up the phone and started calling the cops and I told her not to. And then, so she put the phone down and told me to take everything off and she meant my clothes. I said no way bitch. But she picked the phone back up...and she fucking...bitch...fucking...cunt..."

Jessie trailed off and sniffed and Darren knew he was crying but he didn't know what to do other than sit there. So he sat there, in the dark closet and listened to his friend sniffle-breathe.

"But yeah, so, I'm out of here."

Neither boy said anything and then someone opened the door, pulled a coat out and shut it again. Darren said, "Bob's trying to find me a new place to live. You could live there too."

"I can't wait that long."

Darren didn't say anything and he felt his throat pipe closing itself up and his face go tense.

"Oh yeah, and as a goodbye present to the bitch, I left a half a bottle of rat poison in her cat's food bowls this morning before they ate. They should be dead soon. Fucking all of them.   Later."

And Jessie left the closet and shut the door. Then he left the orphanage forever.

Jessie hadn't known that Darren loved the cats with all his heart.

Darren started to shiver.

Then he slammed his head against the wall of the closet as hard as he could. He did this twice more and the third hit split his left eyebrow open, blood seeping down to his open mouth. He cried and cried with his head aching and just kept crying, clawing away at his face, and his insides cramped and as he squeezed the tears out and gasped for air, he whimpered up imaginary conversations with Jessie. Pathetic, in the dark, he begged Jessie to do whatever he wanted, but just not to hurt the cats, because even though he'd never told anybody, he really loved the cats and they didn't do anything to anybody. But Jessie wasn't there to hear him begging and crying for Sneakers' life. Darren asked him not to leave and told him that they would get Ms. Bitch in trouble, so he didn't have to go. Please. But Jessie wasn't there for that either.

Darren was alone all evening in the dark, all mixed up with something like hatred-loss filling his head. He didn't know who to blame. And he didn't know what to do. He knew that his only friend was hurt, his friend had left, and everything he loved was dying.

He couldn't bring himself to leave the coat closet, scared to see the plethora of cat-friends dying all painful, outside. So he stayed where he was, wrapped himself up in one of the coats and cried himself to sleep trying to think about TV. He did not brush his teeth. He did not go to bed. He did not take his little blue pill.

+

Darren was eight when his mom died. It was a closed casket funeral because she had been shot in the face by a sniper. This was a very strange way for her to die being that she was not in a war at the time and not the president of the United States of America and not a black person human rights activist. She was just a regular Jane Doe, driving late night on the express way home from work at the hospital.

Darren's Dad sipped on a fifth of whiskey as they drove home from her funeral. He drove slow and both boy and Dad were silent, staring through the windshield at the road ahead. They both had very similar droopy sad hound dog faces on.

When they arrived to their small rural home, they didn't take the time to bring the various assortments of food and flowers into the house. They left all that stuff in the car and plopped onto the front porch chair swing. Darren maneuvered himself under his Dad's arm and his Dad rocked them gently back and forth.

. The sun was setting and the whiskey was almost gone and while still staring ahead towards the fading light, Darren's Dad told him, "You know what the last part of my training was, before I officially became a seal?"

Darren didn't know.

"I had to kill a cow with my bare hands."

Darren didn't say anything, but actually this information impressed him.

"I hated it. But I think that I had a duty."

Darren's Dad's eyes went wishy-washy. Darren hugged him tight around the waist and his Dad rubbed the boy's back softly. Crumbling-hopelessly, he tried to hold back the tears in front of his son. No use. Together they rocked like that until the sun moved away for the night and the whiskey was all gone from the bottle. Down deep under everything else, "At least we have each other," they thought.

+

Darren's rich foster dad or as Jessie called him, Yuppie-Dad, decided to run for governor when Darren was about fourteen. This left Darren home alone often, because Yuppie-Dad had to travel all over the state to make everyone like him, and Darren's Yuppie-Mom was usually out doing aerobics/shopping. Darren would spend most of his time after school searching on the inter-web for Sammyman. Also, he of course watched <u>Saved By the Bell</u>. This seemed to be the constant in his life, with houses and guardians being the variables. Although, now he claimed to watch the show for ironic reasons. Jessie thought that this was bullshit. And he *said* that this was bullshit, with red glazy-roly-poly eyes, as he sat on a big/huge cloud-like basement sofa.

"Bullshit. You're still fucking in love with all of them. Every single bitch-and-ass character."

"I just like to laugh at them."

"You always did. Nothings changed."

"No, before I was laughing *with* them."

"They are characters made to be silly who do silly fucking things, if you laugh at them, you laugh *with* them."

Darren's Yuppie-Mom then bounded into the basement in spandex, fresh from aerobic/yoga class.

"Hey hey boys! How we doing?"

Jessie said, pretty good and Darren didn't respond at all.

"Good good, can I get you anything? You boys thirsty, you hungry, we've got some hot pockets?"

"I want a hot pocket."

"What about you Darren, you want a hot pocket?"

Darren said, "O.K."

Right after Yuppie-Mom left the room to prepare two hot pockets, Jessie said to Darren, "You're Yuppie-Mom is kind of *bangin.*"

Darren shrugged and nodded his agreement.

Jessie made a crinkled face, "Man, you're not supposed to fucking *agree* that you're Yuppie-Mom is *hot.* Gross."

Darren thought about this, "She's just my foster Yuppie-Mom. It's not like she's my blood Yuppie-Mom or anything."

Jessie leaned back, "Yeah. I guess. You know, Bangin Blood Yuppie-Mom would be a good name for a rap group."

Darren made a smiley face.

+

When Bob showed up at the orphanage, the day after Jessie had left, the place seemed to be empty. He knocked and knocked and then just opened the door, upon realizing it was unlocked. He walked in and two potential foster parents for Darren walked in right behind him. They were old friends of Bob from his college days. Bob had told them of Darren's dilemma and they wanted to help. So this was supposed be the first time they would meet Darren. They were dressed in hemp pants and a flowered skirt and what seemed to be homemade tie-dye. The orphanage had a death like smell that day. This was partially caused by the dozens of dead cats flowered about the carpet.

"What on earth?" Bob was reasonably confused and grossed out. Him and his companions walked through the house looking for signs of life. But all of the kids had left and Ms. Bitch was not responding to their calls of, "Hey, anybody there?" They stepped over cat after cat, and tried to guide their footsteps in between the coughed up blood and cat insides. They held their noses.

Ms. Bitch was lying on her bed. She was as dead as her cats and covered in either cat, or her own vomit-blood. There were big bottles of Drano and rat poison right next to her.

Upon this discovery, Bob and friends decided to exit the house in order to find a less disgusting place to call the police. But just as they were about to shut the front door, Bob stood in the doorway and called out one last time, "Is anybody here? If you are, it's O.K. to come out now!"

Then the closet door opened real slow-like and Darren meandered out. He was covering his eyes with both of his hands and shaky-mouse-like, he asked, "Bob? Are the cats all dead?"

+

Darren was pining over-infatuated with-attracted to-filled with lust over- day dreaming about-not sleeping because of-making up fantastic imaginary situations in which the earth opened up causing him to outstretch his strong hand and bravely save, Sammyman. He'd only talked to her that one time on the Web-o-matic and the conversation could have been better, he felt. He had already typed a lengthy list of explanations in case he ever met her again on the Highway-to-Info . His plan was to copy and then paste these pre-written statements into the conversation, so he didn't even have to type. That way he couldn't possibly screw it up, if only he could find her again. His prepared statements included:

-Hang on before you sign off. I'm not stalking you.

-I'm coming clean, my name is Darren and I *also* sometimes pose as something I'm not on the internet.

-I know its strange, but I've never met anyone else who does it, I think we are probably a lot alike?

-I'm really not gross.

-I'm really not a pervert

(although he wasn't really sure about that one)

-The thing is, I'm just a kid and I say that stuff to get people's guard down, because then they think it's ok to tell me some really weird stuff.

-Don't you think it's weird that people will type what they won't say?

He pictured her to be *his* age and pretty and he figured he would never ever find out. She probably deleted the screename right after she signed off, the last time they talked, so as to forget that she had ever once ventured in (even if just as a spy) to the world of weasel-eyed sex-typing perverts. Leaving him to ghost his way through the chatrooms of hell for an eternity, searching and searching for her.

And still he dreamed. He imagined every girl at school to be her. He just wanted one girl he could talk to, and he knew it had to be someone kind of open minded. Or at least *trying* to be kind of open minded.   And Sammyman was at least *that.*

+

I dreamed that I met a cartoon bunny from cereal commercials. Except, I think he was Japanese, because sometimes his speech was in Japanese, so I don't know a lot of what he said, but somehow I knew that he was explaining to me that the reason Japan has all the best technology is because long ago they invented a time machine. And they took that time machine to the future and then returned to the present with all kinds of video games, and cameras and stuff like that, and then I remembered Jessie and Ms. Bitch and I asked the bunny if I could use the time machine and I explained the situation and he said that the only way I could possibly save my friend was to go back in time and kill Ms. Bitch, before she hurt Jessie, and so I traveled with him back in time to the orphanage and she was asleep, and at first I played with some of the cats and was happy to see them and then I saw the Japanese Cartoon Bunny pouring the rat poison into the Drano, and then I was the Japanese Bunny and then he was telling me that this was going to be hard but that it had to be done, for the sake of the cats. But more importantly for the sake of Jessie. And we walked into her room and he grabbed her and she woke up and she started fighting and screaming, and I couldn't get the bottle into her mouth so he grabbed it from me and told me to hold her down and then he said something in Japanese and struck the bottle deep into her mouth and I tried not to look but I was holding her down the best I could and she was choking and-but swallowing and I was about to cry, but Jessie was there, like coaching me, going, "Not many people...would do this for *me*." And it made me feel almost like a hero or something and then it was over and I saw that the Bunny was writing something and I asked him what it was and he said that it was a suicide note and that he had copied her handwriting from a post it note by her phone. And I thought that it was a good idea. Then he told me it was over and I should go back to sleep, but then I remembered that I had slept in the closet so I decided I should go back in there so no one would notice that I was time traveling. And as I wrapped up in a big-soft-coat I fell asleep.

I don't know.

It made sense at the time.

And then I woke up to Bob's voice and smelled a really bad smell. I guess I kind of hoped my dream was real and that I'd saved the cats, but that smell made my stomach so swirly-scared that I pretty much knew what was waiting outside.

+

Remember that kid? Darren barely could. This kid was the one at the first gang meeting who wasn't gothy or thuggy or anything at all actually. He was uninteresting to Darren. That kid committed suicide with a rope and gravity. Darren wasn't sure how to feel about it once he'd found out (and then was reminded who the kid actually was). The news had a strange effect on him, considering all of the people who had died in

Darren's life. Even just considering all of the people Darren had *killed*. He wondered what the kid's story was. Darren wondered if the kid's problem with life was that *nobody* knew his story. Or maybe too many people knew his story. Or maybe there wasn't much of a story at all. Darren decided that there was no way to know exactly what had made the uninteresting kid decide that existence was a minus. It made Darren feel kind of bad though, no matter what it was. Just that somebody gave up.

+

One day when he was fourteen, Darren entered into the Worldly-Web at the empty-yuppie-nest. He still signed on as Prettybaby10 just in case the mystery girl behind the Sammyman curtain was signed on under a different name. Maybe she would reprimand him for being up to his old tricks again. Even to be reprimanded again would be better than never hearing from her at all. He bounced from chatroom to chatroom looking for her. In a chatroom called Kinky Kats he had this conversation with a stranger.

Prettybaby10:what r u into?

Sicilo40: I want to put someone in an oven.

Darren read this twice.

Prettybaby10: really?

Sicilo40: Yes.

Prettybaby10:y?

Sicilo40: I just want to strip someone little, slowly, push them in and shut the door and see the look on their face as they watch me turn the heat on higher until their flesh starts to...

Darren turned off his computer.

He stared at the blank screen kind of shaky-scared.

What the fuck? He thought.

Why ovens?

Where does this kind of thing come from?

Does one just think of this and then find themselves with an erection? Why torture? Darren wondered if God had rigged this man's penis to spring up for things like elaborate burning-murder scenarios and only for things like elaborate-burning-murder scenarios. He sure couldn't help the fact that *he* got erections from thinking about pretty girls. He hoped that this man *only* got erections from *thinking* about putting people in ovens. And this was all assuming that Sicilo40 was a man.

This was very strange.

Darren picked up the phone and called Jessie's cellular telephone.

"I think I want to try marijuana now."

"I'M ON MY WAY!"

Jessie wasn't as excited as he sounded. Not about smoking Darren's brains out for the first time anyway. He responded so loudly because he was driving; fourteen years old on the express way, and felt like his vision was in slow motion. He had a joint in his mouth and he had just taken a hit from a nitrous oxide tank he had stored in his glove compartment. It was all throbbing pound-pound-pounding from his perspective and he was about to swerve around a car. And that's when Darren said he wanted to try marijuana over the phone.

Darren still felt weird about the oven guy when Jessie showed up with hard alcohol breath. Jessie grabbed him by the arm and pulled him to the car and Darren said, "you don't have any?" And Jessie drove them to the warehouse and slurred, "I just ran out, here you can have these if you want?" He handed Darren pills and Jessie wasn't sure what they were and so Darren passed and Jessie ate them like cookie monster.

The warehouse was bangin. The gang was working out very well. Jessie now had it decked out, ninja-turtle-movie Foot Clan style (although he swore to Darren that the name of the gang was not The Foot Clan, the gang had no name, although he agreed that if the gang were to have a name, The Foot Clan would be a cool name for their gang or at least for their rap group to have). There were skate ramps, arcade games everywhere, tons of kids smoking cigarettes and loud thuggy rap music accelerating everything. Just as their parents had feared.

In the corner, thousands of dollars worth of coke was being cut on a table by a gothy eleven year old boy in lab coat and rubber gloves that were way too big for him. Adult clothes on a kid. He was guarded by two twelve year olds. One was armed with two uzis, the other had an assault rifle, terrorist-style. And behind them, the punk rockers cooked crystal meth. If they exploded themselves dead, fuck it. That's just how they thought man.

"See, I went to the doctor cause I was depressed, I think from doing too many drugs. (This was Jessie talking) And I said doctor I'm depressed and so he gave me these pills and I don't really feel any better, but I do feel a lot weirder, I think. Like above myself."

They reached a table with some huge stoner-boner mountains of marijuana on it. Jessie said, "Where's the good stuff?"

"All gone. Sold it this morning," said a thuggy, sunglasses-wearing-in-a-dark-warehouse, child.

"To who?" Jessie snuffed up some fresh meth from a mohawked kid. Jessie did not look well.

"To Stan and Ted and Rodriguez."

Jessie grabbed Daren's arm and off to the Underage Mobile they went.

Jessie kind of wanted heroin so they stopped at a very nice house to get it and Darren was wondering less about the oven guy and more about the idea of *gateway* drugs.

Jessie said, "I will only be a second." Then he inhaled a balloon of laughy gas and Darren watched him stumble all giggle-floppy to the door.

Darren was thinking, "Jessie has been there since the beginning."

+

One time, at the orphanage, a little boy, who would be

described as black by someone who wasn't black, called Darren a nigger. This confused Darren because he thought that the word nigger was a bad term used to badly describe black people in a bad way. And yet Darren would be described as *white* by someone who wasn't white.

Ms. Bitch said, "We don't say that word, Joey."

"Shut up Bitch!"

"We don't say shut up either, Joey."

Darren didn't say anything. He had heard black people call each other the word, but when they did it, they seemed to do it in a smiley-face way. Plus it was said slightly different with an "*a*" sound instead of an "*er*" sound. Darren thought that maybe, since the word nigger was a racist word, the boy was calling Darren a racist. Darren grew scared. He didn't want to be a racist.

In actuality, Joey called Darren a nigger because Joey had been called that a lot in a *bad* way, by a *bad* white foster mom, for a couple of *bad* years of his life. This caused Joey to occasionally and accidentally refer to people as niggers when he got frustrated with them. It was a slip of the tongue that happened sometimes when he got upset. Even when he was talking to white people.

Joey had wanted to watch the TV and Darren of course did not respond to his request, being that he was zombie-fied by the show he was watching. But after Joey called him a nigger, Darren woke up and gave Joey the TV because he was scared of being thought of as racist. After getting the TV from Darren, Joey thought that maybe calling white people niggers was a good way to get them to do things for him.

+

Darren couldn't always remember to take his pill. He was just a kid. Sometimes he would fall asleep without even knowing it. This didn't mean he was necessarily going to

rampage everything in a punk kind of way or murder
something. Sometimes he had dreams and didn't kill anyone
at all.   Those were good nights.

+

When Darren rode to the police station with his lawyer
Bob and his soon to be Hippie-Foster-Parents, Bob asked
Darren some questions.

"Darren, did you see Ms. Bitchington?"

Darren wasn't sure how to respond, but he thought
back to his dream and the time machine and answered,
"Yeah."

"Are you O.K.?"

"I don't think so."

"Do you know what happened?"

"All the cats are dead."

"Yes. I think Ms. Bitchington killed them."

Darren was thinking about Ms. Bitch wanting to have
sex with Jessie.

"Ms. Bitch is crazy and mean."

"I think that sounds about right, but Darren, Ms. Bitch
is dead now. You know that right?"

"I figured."

"She committed suicide, I think," said Bob.

After that, Darren didn't say anything. Darren's new
Hippie-Parents didn't say anything. And Bob didn't say
anything.   It was a quiet car ride for the rest of the way to the
police station. Bob didn't explain the Hippie-Parents to Darren
and Darren didn't ask. Also, Darren didn't explain that he'd
had a dream about a Japanese Cartoon Bunny that may have
caused him to kill Ms. Bitch. He didn't want to go to jail for
forgetting to take his pill, but that is not the main reason he
kept all silent. He didn't want to have to explain about Jessie
and Ms. Bitch and how Jessie was selling crack and cigarettes.

Because he thought Jessie would be embarrassed about Ms. Bitch molesting him. Also he didn't want Jessie to have to go live in a jail cell for exchanging drugs and money. So Darren sat in the car and he let his eyes go saggy. The sun burning in through the open window, plus a warm wind made him realize how tired he was. He had not slept well.

+

Naturally, Darren doesn't remember much about his real Mom. The one that wasn't a hippie or a yuppie. This was because she was removed from earth so shortly after Darren had arrived. He knew she had worked at a hospital as a nurse and Darren's Dad always used to tell Darren the story of how they met. One time Real-Dad told him, while Darren watched him chop firewood. He had his burn-your-throat-in -a-warm-way-whiskey on hand in order to help his story telling abilities. This allowed him to get all drunk and talk to Darren like he was just a regular guy at a bar and not a traumatized little eight year old . It is a good thing too. Because if he had been all sober, and able to hand pick his words with caution-thought; this may have caused him to wait until Darren was older to reveal certain stories. And Darren, although he didn't know it, only had one year with his Dad, before Real-Dad would leave earth towards the Real-Mom. Where ever that may be.

Thunk went the axe as real Dad let it fly.

"You know you're Mom, she was a nurse in the war."

"Really?" Darren knew. But he wanted to hear the story again.

"Yup, I'll never forget the day I met her."

Slurp went the whiskey as Real-Dad knocked it back.

"We were heading back from a bunch of shit-fucked old tunnels on the south side. Scraping up and down and through those things was something else. I mean, you knew. You had better of fucking known, right off the bat, one wrong turn in a tunnel check mission, and that was your balls. And so the guys and I, well, we were on top of the world. *Just* cause nobody got wasted in the tunnel. I mean that made it a God damn good day."

Thunk.

"But then, I mean, here is the lesson, don't count your chickens while your guard's down. You have to promise me that."

Darren's Dad looked at the boy and waited. Darren nodded: solemnly promising. His Dad seemed satisfied, slurped some whiskey and continued.

"Cause that's when, straight out of left field, we were cut the fuck down. From the left, from the right, from the trees, I swear to Christ man, bullets were flying up from the goddamn ground. There wasn't anywhere to go."

Slurp.

"People were yelling, "hit the deck," but I knew that wasn't gonna help, I mean they had the high, low and side to side ground on us. We were fucked."

He set up another piece of wood. Thunk. Slurp. Darren's eyes were goggling all transfixed; he knew the story by heart.

"So, I grab the closest guy to me, Dickinson. He was a real asshole, but there wasn't time to be picky and choosey about saving someone, I just grabbed the guy closest to me. And it didn't really matter, because as I was running, leading this kid by the arm, next thing I know, I'm just carrying this asshole's arm, and I'm not sure when the rest of him got separated, and I don't drop it, cause it didn't seem right, asshole or not, I guess I still wanted to try to save a little bit of Dickinson. Or maybe I was just too crazy to think about what I was doing."

Darren knew that his Dad was about to be shot in the story, with a Blammo!

"Then Blammo! I'm fucked, I mean it actually felt like someone tried to fuck me like I was a chick. I mean like they mounted me, looked down, saw that I had a dick, but just pushed on into me anyway. And I don't know how I kept running. I didn't even drop that fucker's arm."

Darren was very proud of his Dad.

"I mean, here I think my balls are gone, imagine that;

thinking your prick could very well be sliding down your pant leg, could damn well fall out by your ankle at anytime, but I just keep on running and *still* don't drop the son of a bitch's arm."

Slurp. Chunk.

"So I collapse back at camp and they pull me into the med-tent. And next thing I know this beautiful girl, a total knockout, is dressing my wounds and they are trying to pull Dickinson's arm away from me, but I won't let it go. I mean, I'm still holding on tight and I grab this beautiful chick by the ass and I pull her close, and I'm crying like a little girl and I tell her, 'Tell me I still have my junk, nice lady, is my junk still there?' And I let her go, but I don't let go of the arm I'm holding until she pops up to me and says in the sweetest candy-voice-whisper, right in my ear all nice and soft, 'Don't worry Baby, you are *more* than O.K. down *there.*' And I finally breathed out relief and let go of Dickinson's arm thanking God for this hot little angel who was saving me and of course for my *shit* still being in tact. And that hot little angel with the sweet voice and great can. That was your Mom, Darren."

Thunk went the ax.

+

This is a letter that Darren received from Jessie, after Jessie had run away from the orphanage, and Darren had moved in with some hippies. It was the first Darren had heard from Jessie in a long while.

For eyes of Darren only,

What up mother fucker. Don't ask how I found you, because I'm not there to answer you and plus I don't want to give away my tactics. Where are you going to school now? I need to get out of this school, it's totally lame. I just moved out of Yims' place (the guy I used to get the crack from). It's cool though, I'm surprised they let me stay as long as they did. All I did was play video games and smoke their crack, and eat their food. I smoked so much crack man, it was retarded. I was just all feeling all weird after the whole Ms. Bitch thing.

I heard she committed suicide. Did she really? Was it because of the fucking cats?! That would be amazing. I made a bunch of cash and Yims and his friends gave me a bunch more, just cause they care. And I have figured out how to get money and I have an apartment. A bunch of fucking crack dealers care about me man, more than any other old person I've ever met. Its kind of funny. I'm out on my own and it's awesome. Life's totally insane in the membrane. That reminds me, you need to listen to some of this music that Yims gave me. It's bangin and shit. You will probably be hearing from me soon.

Hugs and kisses motherfucker,

Jessie

+

Darren eventually accepted that the oven person probably was a real person. A real man/woman living somewhere normal, getting through each day, dreaming calmly about pushing other human beings into an oven so it would roast them, all gross. Why not? Ms. Bitch seemed to be all messed up with *sex* stuff. So, why not *oven* stuff? Although the oven thing probably wasn't sexual. Or maybe it was.

Darren thought that the oven person just liked the idea of making people into nothing. Which probably meant that deep down, he just didn't really like people. Of course these were just thoughts, and that was O.K. because Darren didn't really want to know for sure. If kids just turn into a bad head full of ideas, Darren would have rather not known. He already knew too much about Ms. Bitch. Maybe she was just around *so* many kids *so* often, that she forgot how fragile-defenseless they were. Especially when it comes to something like sex-love, which is so fragile-defenseless even for *adults*. Darren hoped that the oven person wouldn't manifest his/her demon-secrets the way Ms. Bitch had. Needless to say, Oven Guy was on Darren's mind a lot. Almost as much as Sammyman.

"Yes. O.K. I understand that you are in love. That's great man. And it's not pathetic at all. The fact that you developed a weird perv-obsession with perv-chat rooms, that eventually evolved into a more specific perv-obsession with a stranger, who seems to share the very same perv-obsession with you, and who may or may not be a thirty year old man or possibly even a chick, seeing that this genderless stranger *did* claim to be both, in the one, very brief quasi-conversation you two lovebirds shared; all of this is not at all weird or pathetic."

Darren looked at Jessie and then spoke to the floor.

"O.K. Now is when I can't tell if you are making fun of me."

"I'm not."

Darren and Jessie started walking through the very crowded hall, bumping into lots of kids who were dressed just the same as them. The only way to tell the difference between people, in a visual way, was to look at their hair and skin and body size. Clothes were no help. They were going to Jessie's locker before art class.

Jessie looked into the top compartment of his locker, on his tippie toes, and continued to talk to Darren.

"I just think maybe you need to move on. Even if Sammyman is actually a chick and is your age and is completely bangin; you two only shared about five lines of dialogue with each other..."

"Six."

"Whatever, six. The point is she clearly doesn't like you. You represent what's wrong with the world to her. It's time to move on."

"I can't."

Jessie grabbed a little eye dropping bottle and Darren noticed Jessie's locker was surprisingly tidy.

"Yes you can. I'm not even suggesting that you like join up with the human race, and actually leave your little yuppie-saved-by-the-internet-stronghold. I don't even expect you to try to talk to real live girls. But for fuck's-sake, you might as well *at least* try to meet someone else on the web. It's fucking *world-wide* man! At this point, unrequited love on the Internet is lame, even for *you*. Do you want any of this?"

He offered the eye dropper.

"Allergies?"

"No. It's liquid acid."

"No thanks."

Jessie squeezed two drops in each eye and one on his tongue then he shut his locker.

"Let's go to class."

+

One time Darren asked Real-Dad what happens to people after they die. Darren's Dad was cleaning some of his guns at the kitchen table. And of course drinking whiskey. Darren could tell that his Dad was starting to feel better (about Real-Mom dying) because he was drinking his whiskey out of a glass again. With ice. As opposed to straight out of the bottle.

"Well pal, when people die, they go straight to heaven."

The Real-Dad went back to cleaning his double barrel shot gun.

"But *we* don't even pray." Some kids at school had told Darren about praying.

The Real-Dad took his time and a whiskey sip to consider this.

"Well, that's true. We don't."

He started to clean the gun again.

"But it's not about praying Darren. You don't earn it like that. See, we all earn our spot in heaven every day of our lives. Because, you have to understand, this life isn't very good. Oh yeah, it has some great times. But probably most of the time, the bad stuff is *worse* than the good stuff is *good*. And so when we die, God basically says, 'Fuck it, you did what you did with what you had, and it probably wasn't that great. In fact it was probably damn well miserable for you at times.

So here's some heaven for you. You've earned it."

Darren was on his knees in his chair, elbows on the kitchen stable, chin in his hands, thinking towards his Dad. And he said, "Even if you're bad?"

Real Dad held up the gun he was polishing and looked through the sights, examining the weapon. And he said, "Yup. Even if you're bad."

This was good news to Darren. Because he was afraid that he had done something very bad.

+

Darren stared through the windshield, enjoying his eyes, in the parked car, waiting on Jessie. He saw what seemed to be a small pond out in the middle of the concrete road up ahead. He knew that it was like a desert mirage, because the lake was only there kind of, and sometimes it didn't seem to be water, but actually a puddle of glimmery, viscous, liquid-light. He wondered if seeing stuff like that, like eye-brain tricks, was what it was like to be high on marijuana. And then he heard blam-blam sounds, like all kinds of fireworks or gunshots or dynamite. Darren waited, but nothing happened for a couple of minutes and then Jessie bounded on out of the house, carrying a big paper grocery sack. Quickly, he dropped himself into the car.

"Oh man, those guys were coked up."

He rubbed his nose and sniffed in, all loud and hit the gas and spun the tires fast. And Darren wondered if they were in trouble as he struggled to buckle his seat belt.

"Are we in trouble?"

Jessie started flipping through the radio stations, driving like in a getaway car.

"No man, it's totally fine, it was their gun. Everything is cool. They can't trace it to us. Now hand me the tank of nitrous oxide from the glove compartment."

"I think you should wait until we stop driving."

Jessie thought about this.

"You're probably right."

Jessie pulled a joint from his pocket, lit it and continued driving.

"I thought you said you were all out?"

"What?"

"The whole point of this journey was so you could find me pot to try."

Jessie accidentally rubbed and screeched the car against a another car which was parked on the side of the street . He was speeding, speeding, down the road.

"Oh right! Yeah, you don't want this."

Darren thought for a second.

"Because it's dusted?"

"Yes. Because it's dusted."

Jessie started geek-giggling out. Darren wondered if he should take the wheel, but he had never driven a car before in his life and he was scared to try. He looked in the sack Jessie had brought from the really nice house they had just left. Their were several square shaped big plastic bags filled with brown. Darren asked what the brown stuff was.

"That? How many bags is that?"

"Five."

"*That* is fifty-thousand dollars worth of really good heroin."

"I just wanted to try pot."

"Yeah. Well, then that's not for you, is it?"

Speeding and swerving, too late, Jessie smashed an older man waiting at the cross-walk with the bumper and sent him twirling and then slamming down to the sidewalk with a snap. Darren made an inaudible, dry-heavish type sound as it happened. But it happened very quickly and Jessie kept driving, very fast down the road. Darren was turned around, watching and watching the scene fade out into a distance-blur. Two people were running to the crunched old man and getting smaller and smaller. He wasn't sure if Jessie was consciously trying to get away or if he even realized what had happened.

"I think you just killed that guy."

"Oh I killed *all* of those guys. Don't worry about it man, nobody's coming after us."

"Jessie we have to go back there, you just hit someone with your car."

"Really? When?"

Jessie groaned and put his head in his hands and started rubbing his eye's trying to remember if he had hit someone, still speed-swerving along. Darren grabbed the wheel and spun it away from the tree. The sudden move sprung Jessie up all alert. He took the wheel back.

"O.K. The thing is that even if I did hit someone back there, which we are still not sure about..."

Darren was sure.

"...we can not possibly go back. There is nothing we could have done to help, that other people won't do, this is our fucking turn anyway."

He swung the car onto a dirt road. Darren didn't argue as he sped along side a heavily wooded area. And he didn't even have time to argue, when Jessie fiercely pulled off into a hole in the woods, digging through branches and shrubs and finally air-bag-slamming into a thick set of bushes. Jessie seemed pleased.

"Welp. Here we are."

They grabbed the bag of heroin and Jessie's tank of nitrous oxide and a bag of balloons, and Darren followed Jessie deeper into the woods.

"Jessie. I think we should go back. That guy could seriously be dead."

"Look. What I did was, arguably, pretty bad."

He stopped walking to explain things to Darren and to fill up a balloon.

"I made a mistake. That's it. I *accidentally* maimed someone, O.K. It was a *mistake*. But going back there with a stolen car, too young to drive, fucked on all kinds of stuff, with lots of heroin on us, would not have helped that person I hit.

It wouldn't have made them feel better, and it wouldn't have brought him or her or whatever, back from the grave. The only thing that us going back there would have accomplished is us being locked up. And once again, a jail term is not going to help me, you, or the guy I squashed. So yes, according to you, I made a mistake, but going back to confess this mistake would be a stupid act of retard/nobility, and a mistake in itself."

Jessie sucked in the contents of the balloon and fell on the forest floor all giggly. Then looked up through the trees towards the sky and said, "Besides, we still have to get you some sticky-icky to try for the first timey-imey."

Darren shrugged.

+

Darren shrugged. And his Hippy-Dad looked at him from the kitchen table, in disbelief. He cocked his head all sideways and made an ugly face in order to display the pain Darren was causing him. Darren was wearing a red, white and blue pair of shorts and one red sock and one blue sock and a shirt with a big American Flag on the front and it read, "Just try and burn this flag!" on the back. Hippie-Dad looked like he was going to throw up.

"Oh, come on Darren! I mean. What the fuck?"

Hippy-Mom chimed in.

"Don't use that language honey, when you use that language it gives the rest of the world permission to shut out your views. Besides, it's flag day at Darren's school."

"Flag day? Darren, that holiday was designed by fascists, did you know that?"

Darren didn't respond.

"They're fucking pushing a simple minded idea of patriotism, just to sell more flags and breed complacency in the masses!"

Darren felt even sillier now in the clothes he was wearing. It had taken everything he'd had inside to put on this wacky out fit, in an attempt to fit in at school. He'd thought he was dressed funny.

"Oh, let him wear what he wants! Don't listen to him Darren, there is nothing wrong with showing a little pride in the system you are a part of, *even* if the system is flawed."

She directed this last bit towards Hippie-Dad.

"Flawed! Fucking flawed! If that's not the understatement of the century! We are talking about a system, built out of slavery, genocide, war, disease, greed; and it still operates on the same..."

"Oh, he is just a kid for *fuck's* sake!"

Everyone paused. Darren started giggling, because he hadn't ever heard his Hippie-Mom swear and he felt incredibly stupid in the outfit he had on. His giggles caused his Hippie-Mom to start giggling too, perhaps still high on her new found power of using the F-word. Hippie-Dad also started chuckling and then did an impression of the Hippie-Mom in a high pitched cartoon-nag voice.

"Anytime you use bad language, it immediately gives everyone the permission they need to tune you..."

"Oh, shut the fuck up."

This caused everyone to fall on the floor, as if they had taken in the contents of a balloon filled with laughy-gas.

+

After Darren killed Ms. Bitch, he had to go through the same kind of questioning as he did back when he killed his Dad. This time it was better though, well, slightly better, because he was not mourning the loss of his Dad, he wasn't covered in blood, everyone thought Ms. Bitch had committed suicide (and not been murdered by Darren), and Bob was there from the very beginning this time. Darren was real sad though, because of the cats. He even started crying at one point, Bob and the police detective mistook his tears as Ms. Bitch tears, however they were tears for Sneakers and Screech and he was scared he wouldn't ever get to see Jessie again. Some kids would talk about running away, but Darren knew that Jessie could probably live life fine on his own at the age of ten. That's just the way Jessie was. For all Darren knew, Jessie might have already moved across the country.

And Darren did kind of feel bad about Ms. Bitch. Not crying bad. He just felt bad that he had killed her for nothing. In his dream, he thought he was killing her in order to stop her from hurting Jessie and in turn hurting the cats. But in actuality, he was a murderer again, for absolutely no reason at all. Thanks to his dreams.

+

One thing that Darren remembered about his Real Mom, besides her being a nurse, was her top two most heartwarming moments. She always used to say that the part in the film, that shows president John F. Kennedy getting shot in the face, right after he gets hit, when Jackie-O crawl-reaches for a big chunk of John F. Kennedy's face, which was knocked off by the bullet; when she, without even hesitating, just grabbed that little hunk of head; it was one of the most heartwarming moments ever in time.

Her second most heartwarming moment was when the Swiss Family Robinson boys return from their journey around the island, with a girl they rescued from pirates, just in time to surprise their mother for Christmas, by emerging out of the dark jungle towards the tree house, singing, "Oh Christmas Tree," in perfect pitch harmonies. "Now that is just heartwarming!" said Darren's Real Mom. It gave her goose bumps on her skin.

+

"Now listen, I am dead serious about this rap group. I could do it, man."

Darren did not respond to Jessie as they walked deeper into the woods, and farther from the wrecked car. He was nervous, because Jessie had killed a pedestrian, alluded to a couple of other murders, and they had lots of drugs. Also, Darren was wondering where they were going.

"I know what you are going to say. I can't rap because I'm white."

Darren was inside-pouty about Jessie's antics, that always seemed to cause Darren the grief-guilt.

"But you know what I'm gonna say when you tell me I can't do something just because I'm white. I'm gonna, straight up, call you a racist."

"Why did you have to kill the cats?"

Jessie stopped and looked at Darren.

"What?"

"I liked the cats. They were my friends. I even had names for them."

Jessie stared, all stoned-dumbfounded, and yet hurt-concerned at the same time.

"I had no idea."

"I know."

Jessie looked down to the ground, and he looked kind of pathetic, standing there holding a balloon full of nitrous oxide, in the dark, all sad and droopy in the middle of the woods.

"I was just..."

Jessie trailed off and Darren wished he hadn't brought it up.

"I know. You didn't know."

Jessie emptied the balloon with a slurp. Then swayed as if he might fall.

"That was like four years ago."

"Yeah."

"I'm really sorry."

"I know."

Jessie started walking again.

"So seriously, I think our rap group should be about being good with blades."

"Where are we going."

"Woods party, so you can try pot."

"Oh yeah."

+

*What happened when Jessie went inside the really nice house
to buy heroin as Darren waited for him in the car:*

So I went inside to see these guys, cause I had heard
from some of the kids in the gang that these guys had the
major hookup on heroin. And I knew these guys. A bunch
of fucking loser yuppie rich-spoiled assholes who I used to
sell crack to, in bulk. They are all like middle aged, and
dumb, lots of inheritance money. And as soon as I get
inside there, I can see that they're all happy-high on
heroin and strung out on coke, and pleased with
themselves for finding such a large quantity of both. And
they look to me like, "what the fuck is this kid doing
here." They didn't even recognize me. It makes me
wonder how many different kids these guys used to buy
crack from.

I ask for some H. And this pony-tail-polo guy is like,
mock surprised. He is all, "Oh-ho, you want to try some
good stuff do you?" And I'm like, "whatever," you know I
just want to get out of there, and this guy is trying to
charge me way too much, and I don't want to do it, cause I
know they won't remember or at least they'll *pretend* to
not remember, but I go ahead and bring up the money that
they owe me from our last transaction and of course, they
act all surprised that this fourteen-year-old kid is telling
them how it's going to be. And I say they can just give me
a couple of hits to go, and we could call it even. This is a
tremendous deal that I have given them.   They owe me a
lot more than that. But this one guy does a line of a coke,
and then picks up a gun that I hadn't noticed sitting on
the coffee-coke-table and says, "Tell you what, you can
suck my dick right here and now, and I will give you a
couple of hits, and we'll call it even." His friends
surrounding him on the couch all let out big dumb laughs.

And I pretend that I'm all pissed off, but I can tell that this guy is serious. So I decide to see where this takes us, and I say, "fine." And he looks at his friends, like to say, "I was just kidding, I ain't no fag." Then he looks at me and is all, "Alright, get over here." And so I walk over to the guy and kneel in front of him, and he pulls his dick out and his coked-up-perv friends drool, all eager-excited to watch me, they are pumped that this is actually going to happen. One by one they start pulling their cocks out too, jerking, and they're all saying, "I got next man." And I'm on my knee's right in front of the first guy's erection and he says, "wait a minute, before you start slurping..." and he leans over to the coffee table to do a line of coke, and he sets his gun down for a sec, all excited cutting the line and I grab it off the table and break his nose with the handle all in one clean motion, before he even realizes what he did wrong.

Then, still on my knees, I calmly shoot each one of them in their face, and watch the blood spatter-paint their dicks. They were all lined up on the couch right in front of me, so it was pretty easy. Then, still on my knees, I did a line of their coke, got up and walked over to their kitchen, washed prints off of the gun, and grabbed the bag of heroin that they had so cleverly hid, right on top of their fucking kitchen counter. Then I did another line of their coke, and remembered that Darren was outside waiting on me in the stolen car. And it was off to a woods party.

+

Darren knew he was in love. Because, it hurt. Right in the stomach area. Everything had become so clear and painfully simple. His destiny was projected up high in plain sight, and it was destroying his existence. His way of wandering around through life as a sightseer was being threatened by an unreasonable-unreachable destination that pestered him, all day (and sometimes all night) long, through an indescribable emptiness, pushing him along, to where and what, he had no idea, but it involved this mystery person, who had finally, undoubtedly, had finally, finally, finally been manifested in the real physical world! Sammyman. Darren was sure he had met her. Not at first. At first he was just hopeful. This was all very melodramatic-traumatic for Darren.

He was walking along the hallway, passing locker after locker, trying not to step on the black tiles, only the white tiles lining the floor. It was a brain-occupying game he played by himself often as he walked. Sometimes it was changed slightly, by trying to not step on the cracks , in between sidewalk blocks. But Darren was walking along and he turned into his classroom, in a head-down-daze, nearly walking right into a beautiful girl. He looked up to see who it was, but he didn't recognize her. She was staring down at his chest, and she said, "Don't you feel silly?" And as if Darren didn't just freeze and have a brain-flash when he heard those words.

He looked down at his shirt, after she walked past him, and he saw that he had a big red stain right on the front . He wondered if his heart had exploded through his ribcage, from the electric shock of it all. But then he remembered the Hawaiian Punch and realized that it had been there for days. He couldn't shake those words though, "Don't you feel silly?" This new girl? Could it be? His mind sprinted and considered how embarrassing it would be if it really was her. He decided then and there that he needed to change his shirt more often.

Jessie was supportive.

"Of course. It must be her. I mean, the girl saw you looking like a retarded person and then she asked if you felt *silly*. Clearly, she must be your long lost internet acquaintance, with whom you shared an imaginary love connection. Things are finally looking up for you."

But Darren's dreams and speculations were driven home in sixth period math class, when the young lady, who was announced to be new to the school, stood up in front of the class and introduced herself as Sammy Normal.

Darren abruptly collapsed and fell out of his desk, to the floor, hitting his head with a thunk. Everyone's eyes went from Sammy to Darren who seemed to be sleeping on the floor on the other side of the room. The teacher asked if he was O.K., but Darren didn't move. Everyone started to crowd around and Darren suddenly popped up like a puppet on strings, all dazed-frightened, he punched the girl standing closest to him, right in the face, and then he tried to reach past the crowd towards Sammy. His hand outstretched, he yelled, "I love you Sammy Man!" Sammy Normal had a terrified face on.

The crowd backed away and Darren's eyes rolled into the far-back of his sockets. His body seemed to remember the head injury it had only just sustained, and again Darren collapsed, smacking his head on the floor, out cold. The Vice Principal had to carry his limp body to the nurse's office.

+

Hippie-Dad said with big surprise-eyes, "You did what?"

Darren spoke quietly to his own lap, "I think I blew the bus garage up."

Hippie-Dad thought about this for exactly thirty-seven seconds and then said, "How?"

+

After all the mayhem and death-drug stuff, Darren and Jessie made it to the woods party. A party is probably a poor description of the actual scene. It was only like ten guys. Kids pounding alcoholic beverages, stolen from parents, like garage-beer, cupboard-hard-liquor, and fridge-wine. There was nowhere else for them to go and be alone with friends, to act crazy and logicless, like there was no point in life, except amazing moments here/there. Often those moments had little or nothing to do with thinking and that stuff. So, these kids would put chemical drinks and pills and smokes and vapors that might hurt them but usually just altered their way of thinking for awhile into their body-systems, like pot.

Darren wasn't sure he wanted to try pot anymore, because he was more concerned about Jessie than he was the oven guy. But then thinking of the oven guy made him concerned about that again. So, he didn't say anything to Jessie about the second thoughts; mostly because of his third thoughts.

Jessie found Stan and Ted and Rodriguez. Stan and Ted were just regular dudes, and Rodriguez was exactly the same except that he had a far more interesting name. In fact,

Stan and Ted could very well have been named something else, equally forgettable.

"Let's smoke. This kid has never smoked before."

"Match?"

"I don't have anymore pot on me."

The trio did not seem happy to smoke out this duo, even with the virgin.

"But I do have a hell of a lot of heroin and a tank of nitrous oxide."

They made happy faces and started to pack a bowl.

+

Jessie wanted to be a good rapper, and decided that reading all kinds of books and novels and poetry would help him become a dope MC. Darren didn't have the patience to read the books that Jessie suggested he read. He liked watching T.V. much better. However, Darren did write a little. When he was little, he wrote Vietnam short stories, inspired by his Dad's wartime experiences. One of them went like this:

The guy looked down at his leg, and it was all bluddy. No one could save him. It was all up to him now. He grabbed his gun and blam blam blam. He shot at the trees and a bunch of yellow guys wearing straw hats fell out (Darren got the impression that the war in Vietnam was like a war against an alien race of little yellow men, he had no idea that Vietnam was a country and the yellow people who lived there weren't really even yellow) . *He started running to save her even though his leg was really hurt bad. A guy in a straw hat got in the way and they faced off. The guy had a sword and all he had was a machette. Cling, clang, cling. They battled and he won, but he didn't kill the yellow guy. He kept running and he saw her there tied up to the tree and the big pot of boiling water. They were gonna dump her in and cook her so there wasn't any time. He threw his gernaide and a bunch of guys went flying out of the way. Then he ran in there and started shooting with the gun he had in his pants. Plus he was dodging around the bullets. He used his machette to save the girl and after all the guys got killed they lived happily ever after.*

The End

+

I'm dreaming that I am finally going to get to spend time with Sammyman and she is glowing all spot-light, standing there, just waiting for me with a sweet smile and the next thing I know, everyone is trying to stop me. The whole school is walking towards me with all these devil-glaring grins on. And then somehow I understand that these are demons coming towards me and that they just wanted me to see her so that it would hurt twice as bad when they pulled us apart again. And I reacted with a punch towards this huge bat thing that was coming at me, which knocked her away and scared the other demons who hissed backwards and so I reached out to Sammyman to pull her past the demons so we could escape towards the hallway and then out of the school. But when I yelled I felt this terrible pounding and it's a fade to black.

+

Darren smoked pot for the first time and Ted and Stan and Rodriguez did whippets for the first time and Jessie did heroin for the first time, through his nose at the woods party. A big fire roared. High school guys were breaking bottles on trees. Jessie was rapping to Darren.

"...the H is in the trunk, with the crank and the skunk..."

Darren layed on his back, geek-giggling up at his friend and the stars.

"...and the glove box is locked, stocked tight with E love..."

A kid fell ten feet from a tree he was climbing, and laughed on the ground at drunkenness.

"...salvia extract, packed up in my pipe.."

Darren wondered for a second if he was really stoned or if he just thought he was, then geek-giggled out again.

"...that shit's got me whacked, and of course I got my knife..."

Rodriguez started to beat-box in between gas/balloons, and Darren thought it was all wonderful.

"...I'm doing about eighty, my eyes feel kinda lazy..."

Ted said, "What's the deal with dealing with deals?" and him and Stan laughter-cracked.

"...the vine smokes maybe, made me kinda crazy..."

Darren was thinking that Jessie was probably the best rapper in the entire world.

"...man could you blame me, for throwing this pointy..."

Suddenly Jessie stopped and looked around, searching the surrounding darkness, just with his eyes. He dropped to his knees and grabbed Darren by the shirt and shook him, like a bad babysitter. Darren's only defense was a fit of silly giggle-gasps like a baby. Jessie talked urgently.

"Darren! This song just popped into my head, and that one line man, they are completely right, we've got to figure out who killed Biggie Smalls or they're going to get all of us man! There's no time, we have to go now!"

Darren was simply delighted with Jessie's crazy-drug-antics and together they cackled through the dark woods, searching for the killer of the late/great Notorious BIG. Kind of for serious, but mostly for crazyness. Definitely for serious too though, definitely.

+

Yuppie-Dad made Darren play baseball. He didn't want to play, because he was no good, but the Yuppie-Dad said that it reflected poorly on him if Darren's life did not appear to be normal to the public. See, that was really the only reason that Yuppie-Dad adopted Darren. After Darren got famous for another traumatizing experience, Yuppie-Dad wanted to step up and get famous for saving the day.

Darren asked Bob if he thought it was a good idea to live with the Yuppie-Dad.

"Well, as far as I know, the guy is nice enough. Maybe a little self absorbed, but I don't really know his wife. I don't know. I would say, give it a shot, maybe see how the wealthy live for awhile. If it sucks, we'll figure something else out."

And so there Darren was. Out on a goddamn baseball field, in the goddamn sun, all goddamn summer. Cursing Bob for not warning him about this stupid baseball obsession. To make things worse, Darren's team made it to the championship game. Darren was of course going to play right field. The only reason he was playing at all was because the Yuppie-Dad used his super-money-powers to make sure Darren kept playing. Yuppie-Dad didn't even go to the games. But he did send an assistant to make sure Darren was playing. The coach hated it. Darren hated it. And the kids hated it. Darren couldn't catch, hit, throw or even pay attention to the game for more than fifteen seconds at a time. He was usually found on hands and knees searching for four leaf clovers when a ball would come near him.

"Goddamn it Darren! If you're not going to play in this game like a player, then you are gonna have to buy a Goddamn ticket like everyone else!" The coach said this to Darren a lot. Darren didn't understand this because it was just a little league game and nobody had to pay or buy a ticket to get in.

The coach had put up with Darren's lack of everything to do with baseball, for the entire season. But not this time. This was the championship. The coach conspired with his best player, a handsome, well-adjusted pitcher who had surely never killed anyone in his sleep.

"Alright. When we warm up, I want you to play catch with Darren. Throw it hard and hit him in the face. He needs to be injured or else I will have to put him in right field."

The star stared all unbelievable-eyes at the coach.

"Look, I'll tell you what: On top of the ice cream you got coming after this thing, I will pay you twenty five dollars to knock that pussy out of commission."

+

Darren was looking at pornography in the Vice Principal's office. After he woke up, the nurse had told him that the VP wanted to see him, and that he was to wait there in his office. Darren waited for ages and ages and he wondered if the computer in the room had the connect-a-web. He decided to explore and although there was no modem and therefore no networking-capabilities, there was a folder marked, "private." Darren clicked and found a pubescent-goldmine of video files.

He watched a video and felt his penis change in preparation for sex, and Darren couldn't help but touch himself. He decided, fuck it, locked the office door and watched dirty movie after dirty movie on the computer, wanting to see a little bit of each, knowing that he wouldn't have another chance to explore this collection.

There were lesbians and cheerleaders and Darren was close to a few seconds of euphoric-gurgling-release when he came across a video of a young girl standing in a basement, hands tied above her head to the ceiling pipes. Blind folded, shaky-naked, squirming. And a fat man, with a black mask stepped up to her and started slapping her hard in the face, with the front, then back, then front of his hand, all bloody, calling her a cunt-fuck and she was screaming and cry/struggling all desperate-frustrated. And the fat man kept slapping her and then he punched her in the stomach over and over again until she threw up all over herself and Darren's erection had shriveled and he horror-frantically turned off the computer and was swearing off all porn and all sex forever and ever, buckling up his pants, when the VP started pounding on the door all, "Open this door, right now, you fucking punk!"

+

One time, when Darren and Jessie were getting high, Darren asked what Jessie thought happened to people after they died.

"We all go to hell. And burn for an eternity."

Darren paused. He had been expecting Jessie to at least

think about it.

"Everyone?"

"Yup."

"Even if you're good."

"Yup."

Darren wasn't sure if Jessie was joking, all funny-funny.

"Are you serious?"

"I'm dead serious."

"...."

+

I dreamed that I was like the real head of the Foot Clan (our gang, not Shredder's) instead of Jessie and not just like the mystery guy (who is really just a glorified mascot). And that all the kids came to me and told me that they didn't want to go to school anymore and I was all cool and wearing a pilot's uniform for some reason, but I said, "Dig. I don't think I want to go to school either." And next thing I know I am at the bus garage and I'm using this snow shovel to fuck things up, all Nirvana like. I'm window smashing and it was pretty much more fun than anything I have ever done in my entire life and I had all these sheets and scissors and there was a gas can and I snipped the sheets to make an elaborate rope-netting of fuse and it stretched and stretched from bus-gas-hole to bus-gas-hole, every single bus was connected and I knew it was gonna be great I even made it like a movie, I said some kind of line like, "Schools Out, you succccckkkkaaaaaasssss!" or "The wheels on the bus go ka-boom" except that the line was probably less cheesy-cool and more nonsensical-trite, something like "Here's to you Mrs. Robinson!" since it was a dream but I don't really remember.

I do remember lighting and running, and I mean like flying, away. All giggles and flapping arms. And I ran and ran until I dropped down behind a tree, nervous-waiting, watching until...**KABLOOOEY**! The bus garage became a volcano and I flew like an angel, to the point where sky meets space and one loses itself in the other, staring down towards the fire below, thinking about how pleased the gang would be with me.

+

On the school bus, Darren said to Jessie, "I want you to do some reconnaissance work for me."

Jessie said, "Somebody's trying to kill me."

The back of the bus where the boys sat at bounced up when the tire hit a curb. Jessie was lacing the joint with coke and the bounce fucked everything.

"Fucked!"

"Jessie?"

"What man!"

Jessie looked disheveled-exasperated, all fifteen-but-fifty-inside year old grizzled, blackness and bags under the eyes, unrested, pissed off.

"Can you still do the reconnaissance work for me?"

"What does that mean, Darren?" All annoyed.

"I want you to learn about Sammy for me."

+

Things, among families, that changed with money :

The kinds of food.

The kinds of furniture.

The amount of talking.

The amount of TVs.

The amount of TV channels.

The amount of fuzziness on the TV.

Remember Joey? The boy who called Darren a nigger.
Joey committed suicide. Darren found this out while watching
TV at the Foot Clan warehouse. He had his own little room
with a couch, where he could smoke pot and watch TV while
Jessie and the rest of the gang did crime stuff. He was
watching a show about serial killers when Jessie came in.

"Remember Joey, the funny kid from the orphanage. He
hung himself."

Darren hadn't realized that Joey had been thought of as
the funny kid.

Jessie left and the show flickered on and Darren was
thinking that the victims of serial killers get a really bad rap,
because they become famous for dying in humiliating-painful
ways. Learning about Joey made Darren feel about the same
way he had felt when the uninteresting kid died. Also, he
decided that suicide people get about the same rap as homicide
victims. Suicide, homicide; it's all just a humiliating/painful
way to overshadow a life's worth of memories.

+

Hoping that the poor girl was an actress, looking down
at his knees, trying not to listen, grossed-out-scared,
frightened of this man who liked pictures of people making love
just as much as he liked pictures of torture (or hopefully just
fake/staged torture). The Vice Principal was a fairly large
young man, with a big gut and goatee to match.   He was the
football coach as well.

"Did you lock this door?!? Did you???"

Perhaps she was just an actress pretending. And they
paid her lots of money, and it was fake vomit, but it was all
very real to Darren. And this man was now leaning down
inches from Darren's nose. Screaming.

"Do you know that the girl you punched in the face got a
black eye."

Darren was sorry.

"I was dreaming."

"Don't say that! Do not say that again! Not here! You might be able to fool a judge and jury and who ever the hell else, but you will not, I repeat, you will not pull this bullshit over on me."

Darren was scared-silent. VP lowered his voice and leaned in close with his fire-breath.

"Do not think that for one second I don't know the truth about you. I've watched you. Dreaming my ass. You sank that axe home that night. You loved it. God knows who else you've killed. You little fucker."

He grabbed Darren by the back of his hair and whispered all quiet in his ear.

"You fucked him with that axe. You murdered him. And you liked it all. You shit. You loved it..."

Darren closed his eyes and was trying to not be there, trying to not feel this terrible sweaty face. Where was this all coming from?

"...did you masturbate that night, you fuck, when you killed your own daddy and cuddled up to his body, did you touch yourself, in the blood..."

Darren broke down in tears, trying to push away this gorilla, all high pitched claustrophobic-screaming, "Stop it! Get away from me!" But he wouldn't let go.

"...you psychopath murderer, pervert, fuck..."

Then the secretary came in and the VP let go, instantly calm.

"Detention, Fridays, for a month."

+

Darren couldn't believe it. He was actually excited about baseball. For the first time, he understood why Yuppie-

Dad thought it was so important that he play. It was the connection you share, with you're fellow players, when together the team makes it all the way to the championship. Everyone seemed excited-nervous and even Darren couldn't help but feel a little bit of pride, even though he knew he hadn't really contributed, he was almost just happy to be part of something/anything successful. Bob even came to the game, and he had a baseball hat on and seemed proud.

Then to top it all off, Randy Selaris, who was *only* the best player, probably in the whole-entire little league, actually asked Darren to throw the ball back and forth, in a warm up style before the game. Normally, the coach made Darren throw a ball up in the air and then try and catch it on the way down as a pre-game warm up, because there weren't enough players for everyone to have a partner.

But not today, Darren tried to contain his smiley-face as he lobbed the ball to Randy. He was thinking he could really get used to this baseball stuff and then Randy threw the ball back as hard as he could and hit Darren smack/crunch in the nose. Instantly bloody-outcold.

THE SECOND PART

"Darren, the bus garage you blew up was in the next town over, it's in the paper."

"So it wasn't even my school?"

"No, it wasn't."

"Figures."

Hippie-Dad looked at the paper.

"No, this is good, maybe that means they will suspect

someone in that town."

"So we don't have to tell anyone that I forgot to take my pill?"

"We aren't saying anything. I'll be Goddamned before you give yourself up to the state, just for dreaming."

Hippie-Mom walked in. And both Darren and Hippie-Dad opted not to inform her of Darren's late night antics. It was Saturday morning and so they decided to drive out to the farmer's market. Darren didn't sleep very well when he was walking in his dreams and so he was all slappy-tired from the night before. He fell asleep in the back seat of the car.

+

Jessie and Darren watched a football game in the student's section. Everyone was standing and so they stood too. Jessie would sit down occasionally because he was all skinny-zombie-white.

"First of all, it's not me they're after, it's you."

"O.K., but did you find anything out about Sammy?"

"Yes, she is a Christian."

He pulled a red bible from his coat all discrete and held it all shaky.

"This is hers."

"You stole it?"

The crowd cheered for home team.

"Yes, I stole it, but you can't have it. This book is changing everything for me. It's cleaning my system. My outlook is completely different."

"You're not on drugs anymore?"

"I've been on heroin for about a month and I'm wheeling and I've eaten some mushrooms. But that's it. And soon it won't even be that. I'm learning so much."

Darren wasn't sure if Jessie was joking. Half-time came and they sat down, during the marching band.

"Did you say someone was trying to kill me?"

"Yes, but I don't know who or why."

Darren saw the Football Coach-Vice Principal down on the field blowing a whistle, all scary.

"Could it be Vice Principal Kremelsen?"

+

One morning at the yuppie-place, when Darren was about fifteen, he woke up ten feet from his bed. On the floor. This was strange because he vividly remembered taking his pill the night before.

+

Darren sometimes fantasized about coming down with some kind of terminal disease. So that he would know how long he had to live. He thought a stopping point and some pain would give him a sense of purpose. Jessie said, "What would you do?"

"I would write down my story I think."

"Well, how about I just kill you in a month. There you go. Now you have a month of purpose to write down your story."

+

At Yims' I killed my first person, so as to pay the rent. I was eleven or twelve. Also, I was working fast food at the time. This was kind of a cover, so I could get an apartment, and get into Darren's school, even though all my real income was coming from selling drugs. Also, I beat Metroid on Nintendo and Yims introduced me to hip hop. Killing someone didn't seem so weird to me. Yims handed me a gun and said shoot this piece of shit, right now, and I

did it. I was high and figured there was probably a fifty-fifty chance that I was doing the world a favor.

+

"Why are you writing it in the third person?"

"What do you mean?"

"It's an autobiography. Shouldn't it be in the first person. I mean you didn't even change your name."

"I didn't do this."

Jessie looking at a thick stack of white pages.

"But this is all about you?"

"I know."

"Look, its not bad, I just think you should try writing some of it in the first person."

"O.K."

"Oh and the sections about me aren't right; I'm rewriting those."

"O.K. But then what?"

"I don't know, just add it all together. Oh, and for the love of God, do not put this conversation in the book."

+

One thing that is similar about Jessie and Yuppie-Dad is that they both had a lot of guns. One might think a gun owner would discourage his teenage foster son (with a history of accidental murder) from using the arsenal. But one of the first things Yuppie-Dad did was show Darren the vault combination and give him an hour long instructional session for each weapon.

"I know I will be out of town a lot, so it will be up to you to hold down the fort. *This* is a Tommy gun, and *this* is how you load it..."

After Darren's Hippie-Parents died, he was dumped back into the brief fame-annoyance that he had, back when he killed his Dad. Bob had managed to keep the trial quiet last time so the fame only lasted for a couple days.   This time, the car crash-tragedy fame lasted a week, on the news anyway. Speculation on Darren was all over the place. Was he a killer, was he a victim, was he the Devil's Son? Why was tragedy following this boy?   Some people thought he should be locked up. One guy on the street called him a murderer. He didn't understand that, because the guy said it all mean and important, like he thought he was telling Darren something Darren didn't already know.

+

Darren was doing coke in the high school bathroom. He worried about a lot of stuff. He was trying not to sleep and he was on drugs; plus, people were after him. And Jessie was off of drugs, but looking worse than ever, all sickly-zombie.

"My teeth are burning in a good way."

"Yeah."

"Jessie, who is trying to kill me?"

"It's either the cops or The Penetrators, or both I think."

"Who?"

"It's a rival gang. Don't worry about them though."

+

After brushing his teeth, taking his pill, and going to sleep in his big Yuppie-Bed, Darren woke up in the bathtub confused.

+

I woke up out of a dream all scared in a weird police car backseat, but no fence between the alien cops up front and me. And they were laughing, taking me to a jail on their pig-planet (they literally did have pig faces in the dream, I'm not just being a dick) and they said they were going to kill me and they started describing what it feels like to be in the electric chair and I'm in the chair and can feel this terrible vibration in my bones and flesh-nerves, all burning. And I'm back in the car and I try to unlock both of the doors to throw/fly myself out. But the doors are locked and something tells me that I have to try and wreck the car, going all crazy. Before they lift off. And they are trying to subdue-stop me by reaching over the front seat, telling me to calm down. I pounce up over the seat, going right for their seatbelts, and the one on the right is trying to buckle me in the center, probably thinking I'm still gonna jump out, so I'm pretending to struggle and as soon as I hear the buckle click, I reach-press the gas with my foot, hit their seatbelts and yank on the wheel, flipping everything and I can feel my stomach turn all weightlessness. And then everything is so quiet-calm, all I can think is I must have died. If only I had.

+

A reporter named Fucko-Mc-Fuckwad once asked Darren, "Did you make up the dreaming defense?" Darren said no, and then years later, at the scene of the car wreck, Fucko-Mc-Fuckwad stuck his horrible-greasy-T.V. face in Darren's red-wet-grieving face once again and asked, "Did you kill both of your parents and get away scot-free?" Darren nodded yes, without really listening to the question. Darren was uninterested in the thoughts/actions of the living. All he really cared about was his dead Hippie-Parents at the time. But Fucko kept asking questions, because all he cared about was making money and looking important on T.V.

"And has it happened here again? Who's next young man?"

+

Darren woke up on a park bench, completely naked-shivering. This was getting to be too much. The pill was not working anymore. He knew he was going to have to stop ignoring this problem. And he had to do it soon, before someone else ended up dead/man-slaughtered. Also, he had to figure out a way to get home, without a whole bunch of people seeing his private parts.

+

"Look, even if it is wrong, why do you think I stay up all night repenting? Besides, I'm sure I saw something in here."

Jessie had just finished a recruiting session. At this point, he had taken to showing a trippy video on a big screen, after drugging the new members with Salvia, instead of the strobe light theatrics of the first couple meetings. They were hanging out in Darren's office at the Foot Clan warehouse. Darren was getting high and Jessie, all sleepless-sandbag-eyes was searching through his bible.

"I'm sorry Jessie, but I do not believe, even for a minute, that you found a section in the Bible condoning a pre-teen prostitution ring."

Jessie kept searching/flipping, all strungoutish.

"I don't know man, you haven't read it."

Darren was concerned because Jessie was pimping out twelve year-old girls to rich/suit guys, who had enough power-money to buy anything they wanted, like for example the souls and bodies of little girls.

"I think it's wrong."

"It might be, but I'm telling you, I've read, almost, this whole book now, and as far as I can tell, God's not overly concerned with chicks. It's like a loophole."

Darren sucked in on the plant/paper smoke, and said, all under his breath, "Oh, fuck God. I don't care what God cares about." Jessie immediately dropped down to his knees and folded his hands, all eyes closed; he talked to God or Jesus, or both at the same time, all silently. He did this as if to answer back, "I do. Listen not to this motherfucker."

Darren wondered if Jessie had been sleeping and eating recently. He wasn't on drugs all day anymore. But his face still looked like an undead-overdose.   Darren asked, "What exactly is it that you do all night?"

+

Jessie's New Nighttime Regiment:

One hour of undisturbed Bible reading, followed by an hour of meditation, five minutes prayer to Jesus, five minutes prayer to God, five minutes directed towards the Holy Ghost.

Sandpaper the skin raw while repeating the Lord's Prayer three times, pour salt on wounds, begin to sing, "And they'll know we are Christians by our love, by our love..." light candles, hold hands over a flame and relive each instance of sin/wickedness, "Thank you Jesus..." blister skin, "Forgive me..." no sleep or food, fasting-worshipping, kneeling, candle-heating a blade, guilty-praising, pulsating, "an all loving god." Bleeding-cutting, cleansing- repent and repeat, holiness striving until the sunrise. Plus, lots of glorious sex.

+

The thing about the little blue pill is that it is as strong as they come. So strong that the doctor warned Darren to never take more than one.

"This stuff will knock you out, and keep you down. But it is strong. Never more than one a night. Not even two. It will kill you. Put you in a coma. Real simple."

+

Darren didn't like being in love anymore. He had Sammy's school schedule memorized. He made sure to leave each class, at least once to go to the bathroom, always taking a path past whichever room Sammy happened to be in at the time. Also, he needed a bump of speed, pretty often, in order keep his eyes all awake-open. After classes he made sure to pass her in the hall. He told himself, this time you will say, "Hello." He also dreamed of saying, "hi," or "what's up?" Sometimes in these fantasies he even considered introducing himself. But every time he walked past, he ducked his head down, because she would be with a friend, or even worse, she would be all alone. Every single time, Darren would split-second go from an excited brain (you can do this) straight into an unsurprised-disappointed brain (you stupid coward-fuck, you will never change).

Darren was walking to the bathroom when over the loud speaker, "Darren Fishy, please report to the office." He wondered if maybe Bob was there to take him out of school. He passed Sammy's class, biology. And groaned in his head. She made him feel like a loser, all pretty-unattainable.

He walked into the office and there was some guy in a trenchcoat. Who held out his hand to Darren.

"Darren Fishy, I presume?"

"Yes."

"I don't know what you're playing at. And I don't care. We do not tolerate competition."

The man reached into his coat pocket and pulled a gun with a silencer. Darren crossed his eyes and stared at it, all in his face. That was all he could think to do. Then the guy screamed, all torture and fell to the ground. Darren saw a young boy, wearing black eye make up, kneeling at the man's feet, with two knives. He had just cut both Achilles tendons simultaneously, leaving the man all cripple/useless. And before Darren could figure out what was going on, a punky kid fell from the ceiling, and stabbed the would be assassin in the throat, making him all dead. Then two fat thuggy kids busted into the room with trash bags and washcloths. Jessie right behind them, looking all hung-over/ghost, carrying a bible.

"Clean the blood and get this guy the fuck out of here. Darren, follow me."

"Jessie what is going on?"

"Well it's not just the Penetrators after us, the real honest-to-god mafia is after us. It's almost a bit flattering."

"But why me?"

"They think that you run stuff."

"Can't you tell them that *you* run stuff?"

"Well. I'm not going to do that. But I did get you a date with Sammy."

Darren stopped in the hall and Jessie kept walking. Then, when Darren realized Jessie was not going to backtrack or even wait, he caught up real fast.

"But Jessie, how did you get me a date with her?"

"I told her you liked her, and that you were cool."

"But Jessie, I'm not cool."

"I know, but I had to tell her something. Don't worry, it will be fine, although she is kind of strange. It will be good though. How are you doing on drugs?"

"I need more coke and speed."

Jessie tossed him two plastic bags.

+

Darren stared at his little useless blue pill and thought about his Mom. His Real-Mom and the night she died. He remembered waking up the next morning, still all dreamy. Walking downstairs, in pajamas. His Dad was sitting there, crying in a lazy boy, drinking, staring at the wall; he was silently asking it questions. The wall had no answers.

"You're Mom died last night, Son. She was shot and killed by a sniper."

Darren looked down at his feet and waited for his eyes to start raining.

"I was afraid of something like that."

No one heard Darren say that.

And so years later, he was there with the useless blue pill, ready to go to bed, but afraid to dream. Thinking about Mom. God only knew what acts of murder-destruction might follow if he were to go to sleep. And Darren wondered if that meant it was *God* who was controlling him, when he was all unconsciousness-zonked out. Because Darren certainly had no say in his actions. He picked up the phone.

"Jessie, do you have any drugs?"

"I've stopped that Darren. I only need God now."

"I know, but I can't sleep."

"You wan't sleeping pills?"

"No, I mean, I cannot sleep. Or I might hurt more people. I have to stay awake."

"Alright, I'll pick you up."

+

Darren's New Regiment:

One line of speed in the morning, a bump every couple of hours until evening, then one more line. Two lines of coke at sunset. Wait an hour and a half, take one Aderol, crunch up Ritalin and snort. Smoke a bowl, twenty minutes and then one more bump, watch tape after tape of Saved by the Bell, more coke, surf the web-a-net until dawn and then repeat.

+

Bob picked Darren up after the car crash that killed the Hippie-Parents. Darren's face was all broken-sad.

"Bob, what's the name of that reporter guy?"

"Probably Fucko McFuckwad. Darren, that guy sucks."

Darren made a smiley face.

"Yeah."

Darren wondered how much of his time was spent smiley faced and how much time was spent frowny-faced and it was this line of thinking that turned his sad face back on. He was thinking about the Hippies.

"Bob, what happens when we die?"

Bob thought about this question for exactly fifteen seconds and then,

"I don't really know Darren."

"But what do you *think* happens?"

"Well, most of the time I think that the person who dies and all of the memories they have are gone, but that they live on through other people's memories. I don't know if that makes sense."

"So everything just stops for the dead person."

"I don't know. But it's one theory."

Darren tried to imagine not existing at all, and the idea of total nothing seemed lonely-scary.

"I'm not sure I like that."

"Sometimes, I don't either. But then I think, if you aren't around to *feel*, than you won't be able to feel bad, or scared, or lonely or anything else that might seem bad about not existing."

"I guess, but I think I'd rather just go to heaven."

"Yeah, me too. And shit, maybe we do. Let's just hope for that then. And if there is a heaven and we do get in, lct's hope Fucko McFuckwad doesn't."

Darren made another smiley face that didn't last.

"Bob, where do dreams come from?"

"I don't really know Darren."

"Are they my fault?"

"No."

"But I..."

"It's not your fault Darren."

"Then whose fault is it?"

+

I wake up in a dark enclosed area, really fucking sweaty. First thing I think is that I could go for another

hit and the second thing I think is that I don't know where I am. Then I feel a coat and wonder if I am back in time in the closet with Darren, after the whole Ms. Bitch thing. And so then I'm sweating even more, all panicky.

But Darren is not there and then I feel a door in front of me and clothes hanging above me and I remember that I am in Sammy's closet and that I am supposed to be spying on her for Darren. Then a light flicks on and I realize I can kind of see through the blinds of the closet.

She walks in and I wonder why the fuck I agreed to do this. Why and how did I end up hidden here? How long have I been here, passed out? But Jesus Christ, she is hot. And I'm so nervous and a little voice says that a hit would make me feel better about all of this. She won't go in the closet. I'm telling myself. And I'm unzipping my kit all tucked in the corner, hoping that if she opens the door I might still go unnoticed.

She doesn't seem to hear me flicking the lighter under the spoon, and I know this because she starts undressing. Oh my God, I'm thinking. Her shirt is coming off, button after button and I'm understanding Darren's infatuation completely and I'm trying to watch and still suck the heroin up through a cotton swab into a syringe and her skin is so pale and smooth and I can't look away as I am tying off, just praying for her to unclasp her bra, with everything I have, I am asking the forces of nature and God to please, please, please let her take her bra off. And as she reaches for the little hook, I prick my arm, and gasp a little as she unclasps and turns around and faces the closet as she lets it fall, like she wants me to see everything; soft chest and I'm pushing the hammer in, even if she is headed right for me, I can't stop now, I want her to find me so that I might be able to touch her, and I feel the chemical rush going through me as she lets her skirt fall and she grabs a book and starts flipping through it and when she finds the page she wants, she sets the book down on her bed, open to her passage, and I'm probably glowing I'm so high. She is standing over the book, I think it's the Bible and then like an angel, she slides her underwear down her smooth white legs. And I'm out of my body and mind, from her beauty/nakedness and the drugs and I'm rubbing and unzipping myself, as

74

she is mumbling something, and she starts touching herself gently too, whispering, I think it sounds like, "forgive me" her fingers are tracing her curves and I am a horrible person and wish I could be her fingers and she is going to catch me, and she is rubbing and squirming, getting louder, "Please, please forgive me, I'm so sorry..." her moaning is so sweet and I'm just so amazed-high, and excited and she pulls something small and metal from inside the Bible, still masturbating with one hand, eyes closed, and then digs the metal into her stomach and gasps, "Forgive me God..." tears, but her moans are even louder now, and I cringe as she cuts again but I understand her; oh my God, the pleasure, and the pentenance-pain *for* the pleasure, simultaneously, I feel her rush-release, the high she feels when her guilt pours out through the flesh wounds and it is too much, she is too much and my erection is too much, and her moans are everything and I'm out of the closet door before I can stop myself, in tears, "Please," I'm saying as I pull my shirt off startling her, "I need you..." and my pants too and I kneel at the foot of her bed, naked, and she is beyond shocked, but so close to release, covering herself, but still touching herself, so close and I'm touching her skin and the blood from her cuts, and I pull her down to her knees, face to face with me, begging, I hold my hand up, wet with her blood, "I'm a terrible person, please, I need this, please..." and somehow, like a fantasy, her eyes change, from scared-embarrassed to knowing me, and she seems to understand what it is I need and who I am and she takes a hold of my hand and touches it to her face "Ask him to forgive you" and before I can, she cuts me down the palm of my hand and the sting is release, "forgive me," I whisper and feel her take a hold of my erection, she is smiling and kisses me, and I close my eyes tight and moan feeling her cut my chest, stroking me with her other hand, and the pain and blood is my guilt, "Oh God, forgive me." And I am on top of her and my life is changed completely. And I can not tell Darren about this.

+

"What am I doing?"

The days and nights and moments were all running together for Darren, since he swore off sleeping.

"I'm taking you to Flip-a-Quickers Pizza. You have a fucking date with Sammy."

Jessie still drove underage, and still drove crazy, and still committed all kinds of crimes, and still said words like fuck, even though he started practicing Christianity. When Darren asked about the contradiction, he claimed that he made up for it with all night repent/cramming sessions. And then he'd say, "Maybe you should think about repenting?" And then Darren would always drop the subject.

+

In detention with the Football VP, Darren had lots of trouble staying awake. In fact, Darren had lots of trouble with everything during those sessions.

"Tell me how much you enjoyed it, you little fucker."

This guy, who desperately loved to mix up sex with murder-torture, who could easily be the Oven Guy, this man must have had it out for Darren since day one.

"I've been watching you."

Darren hadn't noticed this guy, all lurk-stalking in the shadows. He just wanted to go to the bathroom and do some speed. But no bathroom breaks.

"You can shit yourself for all I care, murderer."

After enough sessions of verbal abuse, Darren was starting to understand that, all in all, it really had nothing to do with Darren.

"How many people have you slaughtered and fucked?"

For this guy, it was all about sex. And yelling at Darren probably made the VP's penis hard. He yelled, probably because he was jealous of Darren's ability to massacre people, all jail free. And probably because this guy was all disgusted with himself. He probably yelled at and tried to hurt Darren, because he was too much of a jerk to yell at and hurt himself. But understanding it didn't mean that it didn't still hurt.

"Don't close your eyes at me, pervert!"

Darren was seeing colors, trying to push time forward to a time when he could do drugs and not be yelled at by gross, self righteous adults. "I hate school," Darren was thinking.

+

"*Where* are we?"

"Why are we here?"

The boys hadn't slept. But they had eaten mushrooms.

"I think we are in a grocery store."

"I think I was trying to be deep."

"I was too?"

"By saying, 'where are we?'"

"What are you talking about, you said that?"

"Why are we in a grocery store?"

"I don't know that question."

"That's a funny phrase to say."

"I don't know that question."

"Not funny the second time though. Just kind of stupid."

"Does this place have a bathroom?"

"Just go man."

Geek/giggling from both boys.

"No, I need more drugs or I'm sleeping/standing."

"What?"

"Self, drug me."

"Why are you talking to yourself, when you can just think it?"

"For your benefit. And also, I want to be locked in a grocery store."

"I feel like we are supposed to be going somewhere."

"There is nowhere to go, but I feel like we should get out of here, like we are being chased."

"Wait, didn't one of us need to go to the bathroom?"

"Why the fuck are we in a grocery store?"

+

I dreamed I was a Vietnamese sniper and I was up on a hill and I had to defend my parents against soldiers like my Dad. So, it was confusing because my emotions were all mind/mixed, and I kind of knew that my Dad was a soldier, and being against him scared me, but I thought that *really* I was a Vietnamese boy and that I had to defend my Vietnamese parents, who were basically yellower versions of my real parents. I was a torn boy/soldier, not sure which side I was on, wishing I didn't have to choose. And then I didn't, because the clouds above me opened up, and I saw God. God was a big/made-of-clouds lion's body with a TV for a head and a picture of a lions head on the TV screen. The head on the screen growled at me and told me not to be confused anymore. He told me that, deep down, I knew which side I was on. I thought hard and then said that I was on my Dad's side and he said, "WRONG!" and that I was on the yellow side, and that I had better kill or be killed. He told me, "NOW!" And so I shot at a moving bright light that seemed closest.

+

"I can't do this, what do I do, how did you make this happen?"

"First thing: are you still wearing tightie-whities? Cause if a girl discovers that you are, she might think it's funny."

Darren checked his underwear and he did, in fact, have on tightie-whities.

"I need to smoke more."

"Too late."

Jessie turned into a parking lot and Darren's stomach went all wiggle/spins and he tried hopeless/crazily to roll a joint as Jessie pulled up to the door of the Quick-a-Flippers Pizza.

"That won't help you with this, trust me. She is a hardcore Christian, so don't tell her you do drugs, cause she hates that."

"She is a *hardcore* Christian?"

Jessie looked at a jagged scar, trailing up his forearm.

"Hardcore as they come."

+

Have you ever wondered why Bob didn't adopt Darren? Well, it wasn't because Bob was scared of the fact that Darren might kill him in his sleep, or that he didn't want the burden of a weird kid to take care of. It was because Bob liked to kissy/touch other *men* instead of *women* and to suck penises and have penises inside of his asshole and put his penis inside of the asses, hands and mouths of other men instead of the vaginas, hands, mouths, and asses of women. Because of this he wasn't deemed fit by society to care for a child. When Darren found out about this rule, he thought it was a strange/silly way of deciding who was going to be good and who was going to be bad at parenting.

+

Darren, all drug/fucked, not sleeping, had all night to do anything. But he found that there wasn't much to do. There was Saved by Bell, which he still watched incessantly. Jessie asked, "How? How can you still watch that stupid fucking show?"

"Because it is a phony/shallow cast of characters, who constantly do stupid/inconsistent/ unbelievable things, that don't really add up, episode to episode, and the whole time, everyone is saying trite line after trite line, cracking bad jokes, learning trite "life lessons," that are either too specific or too general to be at all meaningful or helpful in any other life situation. But all the characters act like they are learning *so much*. So basically; without a doubt, <u>Saved By the Bell</u> is the realest, most true to life show that I have ever seen."

"I guess. But who the fuck wants to watch real life?"

+

I'm naked with Sammy, who could have been Sammyman, who could be completely insane, experiencing an afterglow I've never known. And she is so beautiful, so innocent. So guilt/scarred. Like me. I didn't know I could feel so guilty. And I'm explaining everything to her. How I ended up in the closet. Darren. My drugs. How did this happen, I'm asking her. Thank God she has though, she is pretty-smiling, telling me that it's good that she's found me. And I tell her that I didn't know I had so much guilt inside me. She tells me that it is O.K., and that you learn to deal with it, once you learn to repent all the time, God will forgive you, she tells me. And she is so beautiful, and I am believing everything. She says that sex is just a guilty thing for humans and that's the way it's always been, and I realize that she thinks that I feel guilty about sex and probably thinks everyone feels guilty about sex, probably since *she* feels so guilty about masturbation, but really, my guilt's from murder-gang stuff.

But still the release she gave me was better than heroin. And there she is all naked/soft-curves, inches from me. And she starts telling me about Jesus and how he saves, and that the drugs are really bad, and that I should feel bad about the drugs, and I tell her, please, I can't handle anymore guilt, not right now, and she gently takes a hold of my penis, and breathes in my ear, "It's O.K." And her voice and hand make me hard again, just like that, "You just have to repent." She delicately/barely rubs my erection between her legs, all comfy/moist. "Jesus will love-away your guilt. You could live forever." And all I can do is groan something like O.K. And she is licking my ear, "Do you want to repent?" I'm trying to say yes, as she slides her body against mine and I feel her

warm breasts on my chest and her arm wrapping around my back, "Will you give up the drugs?" And I will do anything for her, "For God," she corrects me with a whisper and I tell her how sorry I am and that I will give up drugs, please. She is inserting me so purposefully/slow, massaging her warm body against mine, she is breathing, "Ask God for forgiveness," And I'm all apologies and suck in air through my teeth, as she cuts a sharp pain across my back, and I'm exhaling the sweetest pleasure-relief as she takes me inside of her completely.

+

"Thank God," Jessie said to Darren.

"It seems to me that if you're going to thank God for all the good stuff, you have to fucking hate him for all the bad stuff."

"Maybe we need the bad to make the good."

"Seems like then, that there should be more good than there is bad."

"There is."

"Maybe that's where we disagree."

+

Darren was thinking that he had better keep watching, but maybe one more hit, start chopping a line, sign on the net-way, and he checked the TV, VHS tape filled with <u>Saved By The Bell</u>, the curly haired dumb looking kid said something all silly-bonkers. Darren did a line of something, maybe coke, maybe Ritalin, he was logged in, his nose stung, must have been meth. Or actually, it wasn't that bad, maybe it was coke. Darren signed on as Prettybaby10. He hadn't done this in awhile, since Sammyman had been manifested in the form of Sammy. But something made him do it. The straight haired blond kid slapped the curly haired kid. He started to pack a bowl. He had his own pipe now, Jessie's old one. Someone asked if he wanted to cyber.

Darren accepted the offer, and as he sucked on glass he wondered if Yuppie-Parents were going to be home anymore, ever since everything went down. He wondered if they had both moved out and just forgot about him. He sprinkled coke on top of the bowl, wondering if it was even a legitimate/real way of taking coke into the system, or if he was just going to burn/waste it. He asked the screen what they were into, hit the bowl, checked the T.V., a big muscle guy talked to cowboy boots and then in came the principal, and Darren remembered he had detention after school and cursed. He sucked in more smoke, and imagined he could taste the cocaine on the pot, or maybe he really could.

Mentor46: I want to in inject human feces into my child.

Darren was thinking, "Seriously. For real. That is what you want to do. This is the act that makes you get an erection," but Darren did not flee this time, he was too fucked up.

Prettybaby10: I don't want to but I have to ask how did u even think of this?

Mentor46: I am a nurse.

Darren hit the bowl and he knew he should have been all grossed-out-scared, but he was too busy just being all confused.

Prettybaby10: y would u want to do that to someone? your own kid?

Mentor46: I don't know, but it gets me excited and horny.

Prettybaby10: but it doesn't have anything to do with sex. thinking about it gives you a boner?

Mentor46: I'm a woman. So no.

Darren hit the bowl and two characters hugged on the TV.

Prettybaby10: do u really want to do this, in real life? for real

Mentor46: No it's just fantasy talk.

Prettybaby10: Really? for real?

Mentor46: Yeah, it's just in my head.

Darren checked the other screen and snorted speed or coke or speed-coke and hit/cashed the bowl. He tried to focus his eyes and wished he could go to sleep.

Prettybaby10: be careful cause i happen to know that sometimes your head will take over when you don't really want it to.

+

"Darren, get out of this car."

"I can't."

"Darren, I have shit I need to take care of."

"I'm paralyzed."

"Darren, I'm so tired, it's going to be fine, besides, you need to stay awake."

"I'm doomed to be alone."

Jessie, all hunched over the wheel, barely able to keep his eyes open, all black underneath, like a goth kid, reached over, opened the door, and kicked Darren right the fuck out of the car and drove away. Darren just stayed all dead-looking in the parking lot for awhile, pretending he actually was paralyzed, he looked up at the sky-clouds and stared, and felt himself drifting off all bliss/pillowy, soft-sleep was on the way, but he popped up, remembering he needed more drugs, he needed to stay awake. He stared at the Quick-a-Flippers Pizza and wished he could have done this with Sammy when he was less crazy and less on-sleepless-drugs. Like, a week ago.

+

Darren ran back to his house. Completely naked. He didn't even remember the dream that had led him there. But apparently, it involved him in a park, birthday-suited. "This is the part people usually wake up from, all relieved-shaken,"

Darren was thinking, as he ran from tree to tree. "But not me. I wake up *in* the fucking naked-dream."

+

This was before I'd given up drugs for Sammy and God.

I'm drug/fucked, and I go to Darren's to see if he wants to get high, it's pretty early in the morning, I was up all night on drugs, running a car, filled with a body and coke and H and I'm feeling great since I'm not in jail, not caught. And I wanted to tell Darren about this idea for a book I had, called, "Working Minimum Wage and Killing People," which would be about how I used to work fast food. And I think there is a car following me. Penetrators, probably. What A God awful name for a gang. What happened to cool names like the crips and the bloods? But I'm not worried about these bozos, I know Darren's Yuppie-Dad's got a fucking arsenal inside and so I kind of hope they try to follow me in.

But I knock on the door and nobody answers. That's no big surprise since Darren basically just lives in the basement, with the computer and the big screen, and the "parents" aren't really ever home. So I walk inside and lock the door and look through the little window, the stalker-car slow-hesitant drives by. And I'm thinking, "That's right, losers."

And I light a joint and start to walk to the basement, and I startle-see the Yuppie-Mom in a really high cut robe, her hairs all wet and I say sorry, I was just looking for Darren, and she doesn't know where he is and in my state I can't help but stare openly at her bare legs, and wonder if she is naked under the robe. And she is approaching and asking if she can hit my joint, which I had totally forgotten about. And I hold it out and nod, surprised she smokes. And she takes it from me, and now I can't help but stare blatantly down her robe, which is too revealing for me to not get an erection. So I do and after hitting the joint a couple more times, she holds it in front of my eyes to pass it back, which wakes me from my locked-in-stare, down her robe-cleavage. But she is not trying to cover herself, so I take the joint and continue to gaze as I hit it, planning to look as long as she will allow me too. And she does me one better and unties the robe and pulls it off. And as she is smiling/pulling my head to her breasts that seem huge, I'm wondering if Darren is home, I'm wondering if this is really happening, but all in all, I'm not really caring about either answer.

+

Bob took Darren to the hospital after Darren's nose got all crush-fucked by a baseball. The Doctor had already finished setting it, and was talking to Darren and Bob, telling them how to go about applying ice. Suddenly, a man in a suit burst into the room, holding a cell phone. The Doctor said, "Excuse me?"

"This is Darren's father on the phone." This suit-man said.

"Wait, then who are you?" The doctor said to Bob.

"Oh, I'm just his lawyer."

Darren took the phone from the suit-stranger and said what sounded like, "Hewo?"

Yuppie-Dad had been informed by his assistant that Darren's nose had been broken right before the first inning of the championship. He called Darren, while sitting in his office with his feet up. "So, you couldn't hold out for just *one* more game?"

+

Yuppie-Dad said, "This is called a rocket launcher. I don't want you fooling around with this one." Darren was kind of bored in Yuppie-Dad's futuristic vault of weaponry. "You're still a little too young for it, and plus I don't exactly own it legally." The rocket launcher looked huge. Darren didn't think he could lift it.

"So, only in a case of the utmost emergency are you too use the rocket launcher. Are we clear?" The Yuppie-Dad looked at Darren and made a serious face, waiting for a response.

"Yes, only during an emergency."

"Good boy. Now, the rockets are up here in this compartment..."

+

"Oh, God."

"Are we still in this grocery store? That is so funny."

"Jessie, I just realized it all. We...I'm crazy and I've always been."

"The aisles don't end. They seem new to me each time. I'm so tired."

"What is the word for this?"

"I think I will live here. It is mellow music for me always. I could sleep on a bed of paper towel rolls."

"Epiphany!"

"I could rap for customers as they get food. This is my calling."

"I'm talking to myself out loud."

"I'm not sure what you mean."

"Jessie, we are the same person, do you understand what I'm saying, different parts of my head! Or your head, I guess. We are the same fucking person!"

"Yes, I know."

"Really? Why didn't you tell me that this is all just in my head, and this grocery store probably is too, am I talking out loud?"

"We are the same person, just because you don't have any other friends, so you emulate me. We're not like the same person in the split-personality-T.V.-movie kind of way, you fucking retard."

"You are just saying that cause you are in my head. Do *you* control me when I'm asleep?"

"Darren. We have not slept for far too long, and we are tripping/twisted, and you watch too much T.V. We are not the same person. You just think that we are because you are on drrruuuugs."

"For sure?"

"I don't know, I guess we both could be the same person. But who gives a shit? Neither one of us would be any less real, right? We would just be *sharing* a body, just like we share a planet. So, whatever."

"Who controls me, Jessie?"

Darren looked all fragile-like, almost in tears.

"I don't know. The ODB?"

That made both boys produce all kinds of tired-face-smiles and lots of geck-out-giggles.

+

"How did you pass the lie detector tests? You fucking cunt-boy-murderer."

Darren wondered what kind of screening process people had to go through to get teacher jobs. The irony of it all was that Darren hadn't ever consciously felt violent towards anyone, until this psychotic vice principal started accusing him for hours at a time, of having a blood lust unparallel to that of a ravenous horde of zombie/cannibals.

After a few weeks of detention-harassment, Darren wanted to kill this man. He wanted to jab a pencil deep into his throat. This big dirty man who made him write, "I will not masturbate onto my fathers corpse." Six hundred times. Darren wanted to grab the overhead projector and swing it with super human strength, down through this man's face/skull, all mush-brain. Then go to sleep. Or do more drugs.

+

I'm going too long without sleep and I'm wondering how Sammy is doing it. I'm thinking she truly is divine. I've lost so much blood, but still, guilty, guilty, guilty. I'm telling her about Darren. She has to meet with Darren. I don't know if I am trying to pass her on. Away. Maybe, I can't do this. It is such a strict regiment and I always feel like I'm fighting myself. But her sex and her God give me a strange comfort-heart sometimes, like everything is right and this world is immortal. And then it's I'm-sorry-guilt, and I'm thinking, "punish myself," and together we mangle each other and fuck and then mangle ourselves to repent for the fucking. Cycles, leaving no time for sleep, and I don't know why I can't do drugs and then just punish myself for that too, and she doesn't have answers for that and I'm wondering if we aren't just fooling ourselves, and then feel guilty, knowing God might be able to read my thoughts. Maybe that's fear. And I start thinking, "*was* I happy on drugs; *am* I happy on God?" I can't remember what I was like before I started feeling like, I am being watched by a superior being.

+

Darren was covering his nudity with a small bush he'd uprooted and a flyer he'd found stuck to a tree. He looked like the birthing surrogate mother for a billboard-tree couple who couldn't conceive on their own. He couldn't fully appreciate this however, as he was running full speed ahead now, finally/thankfully recognizing his neighborhood, almost home. He passed an old man on the road, getting his morning newspaper. The guy yelled something but Darren did not stop. At the moment, he didn't really want to have a conversation with an older stranger.

+

So, as the Yuppie-Mom and I are going at it on their couch, of course, the Yuppie-Dad walks in. His face goes all red, angry and I'm all messed-up, out of it, and feel like I should keep going cause I am really really close, and he is yelling cunt/punk/ungrateful/stop/bullshit, but I just need a couple more thrusts and there it is and seeing me going over the edge, discharging my love inside of his wife seems to push this guy over the edge and he charges at me and I am still recovering from my loss of sex fluid, I only have time to pull my underwear up before I kick him in the balls and hit him in the throat and I start to dress as he gag/coughs on the ground. And the Yuppie-Mom is screaming at me and telling this pathetic hump of tears on the ground that it's just that he isn't ever there for her. And then Darren busts in through the front door, completely naked, coming from God knows where. He looks at us, mortified, and we look at him, all confused. Then he starts to run up the stairs and I run out the front door, all, "Bye Darren," and him all, "Bye Jessie."

+

Darren walked into the Quick-A-Flippers Pizza, all undead/amazed at the swingy-flashy doodad/light/pictures. "Where's the bathroom?" Not waiting for a response he walked into the women's bathroom and in a stall, he snucked coke straight out of a little bag and then back out to find Sammyman. He asked the guy, "Where is she?" The guy made a stumped face, and Darren said, "Sammyman..." and there she was all spotlit/hallowed, waiting. Darren's heart thump-crawled up to his throat, trying to get out. He swallow-gulped and walked over to her, there; looking all perfection/angel. Holding her would be better than everything, better than sleep..

+

I don't know how to say this, I'm trying to work out the words in my head as I'm going down on Sammy, while she cuts herself, this is becoming tired/hard. My body aches all over, I don't remember sleep and no matter how much I hurt myself; myself doesn't learn and I go back and do the same bad shit again. I hurt. My prayers are incessant/automatic, I can't turn it off. And I can't remove this guilt. It's a scary guilt. Vengeful. And she is climaxing and afterwards I'm asking Sammy, "Will you meet with my friend Darren. I think he could use your help."

+

Darren walked to Sammy's table all stumble-wobbles. He was trying to act natural-cool, trying not to say, "I love you. I love you. I love you so much. You are the only beautiful/nervous part of my life right now."

"I'm Darren."

"Hi Darren, I just want you to know that I know you are on drugs and I know you are obsessed with me, and that you have become this way from visiting an internet pervert chatroom. And I just want you to know that God knows as well."

Darren didn't know at all what to say. His eyes were fear and his mouth was sadness and he couldn't move. He felt all stun-gunned.

+

With a light bulb up to his lips, Darren scrolled down. His nose hurt from too much snort/snucking. So, he was trying to figure out how to *smoke* crystal meth, with the help of website directions. Two guys battled for a girl on the TV behind him. One was blonde, one was big. And the Yuppie-Parent's came back. Darren heard voices, kind of.

"I'm sorry..."

"I know ..."

"It's just hard because..."

"Yeah, well you are always..."

"Sorry..."

"No, I'm sorry..."

"I love you..."

Darren felt all gutted. Thinking about Sammy. Thinking about the Yuppie-Parents, all messed up, but married-together, at least. Darren and Sammy Fishy he was thinking. He wanted to cry and sleep and wanted to call Jessie. So, he dialed, not sure whether or not he actually wanted to talk to Jessie. "Maybe I will just hang up," he thought.

"Hello."

Darren didn't say anything.

"Hey Darren, I'm sorry."

Darren didn't say anything, kind of because he was starting to cry.

"I really am. I don't know what else to say."

No one said anything.

"It's O.K."

"Thanks man."

Silence.

"Listen, I just made a great deal with some guy, and I don't know how much longer till everything goes down to hell, but I was thinking about coming over so we could wait it all out together."

"Sneak in through the basement window. Yuppie-Parents are back."

"If you put your faith in Jesus, he will construct happiness. He will reassure you always, that no matter how bad things get, at least there is a heaven waiting."

Darren was staring/drooling at Sammy, but he didn't say a word. He hadn't said a word. But she kept talking as if they had known each other for years.

"You, with your murdering, and your pot, especially. You need to start working on your soul, and fast."

+

"I'm going to fuck you, you little fucking murderer. Fuck you to show you how it feels, you fucking rapist."

Darren was starting to get scared. This was to be his last detention with the evil man and the VP had a tight grip on the back of Darren's neck, as if he didn't want to let it all end. He had been getting increasingly more touchy/feely-rough with Darren. And now the verbal abuse had evolved from strange accusations to violent sex-threats.

"Do you hear me, I'm going to tie you to this desk and fucking rape you, cunt boy."

His fat sweat-face was all clogged up against Darren's. He could feel the VP's mustache hair on his ear. He wanted to disappear into his mind, into sleep.

"Tell me. Tell me you want me to fuck you, you little faggot."

He wanted to throw up. VP grabbed a handful of Darren's hair, and jerk/yanked back.

"I said tell me, faggot."

"No."

He pulled back rip-harder.

"FUCKING TELL ME!"

Darren closed his eyes, expecting to be punched and raped, but the VP's hand let go of his hair and he heard a tumble-plop. He opened his eyes and saw that the VP was on the ground with a big-bloody hole in his face and Jessie was standing right next to him, with a silenced, smoking hand gun.

"I need to talk to you."

A thuggy kid with a basketball jersey on, and a Gothy-trench coat kid grabbed the body of the VP and dumped it into a trashcan, which they immediately started rolling, on its wheels, out of the classroom. Jessie was on his cell phone.

"I don't care, get off your ass and get over here, we need this blood cleaned up yesterday."

Then he hung up the phone, grabbed Darren and started pulling him towards the parking lot.

"Jessie, was the Vice Principal trying to kill me or something?"

"What? Oh, no I don't think so."

"But you just shot him in the head."

"Yeah, I guess I did."

"Why?"

"Well, I needed to talk to you. That guy was a dick anyway."

"Yeah, he sure was."

They hopped into a car and started driving away. Jessie started pounding the steering wheel with his fist.

"Why did you need to talk to me?"

"Because the cops fucking raided The Foot Clan warehouse today. God dammit, I'm so tired."

"How did that happen?"

"I don't know, too many people talking, too many overdoses. Some rich guy got caught with one of the girls. A bunch of shit. But the thing is that a lot of kids were arrested, and they don't have anything on *us* yet, I mean you and me, but I don't know if anyone is snitching. And since they were all kids, my guess is that they will be, probably by the end of the night. Tattling, I mean. Which means we are probably fucked."

"But I didn't even do anything."

"I know that and you know that. But all the members think it's your gang and that you are just this quiet criminal master mind. Remember?"

"I am far too messed for this. I don't even feel real."

"Well, that's good, cause I don't know what's real anymore either and I haven't slept either, but anyway, your date with Sammy is in twenty minutes in case you forgot. So, you'll hang out with her, while I try to figure out what the fuck is going on."

"I can't do this Jessie."

"Well, you fucking have to cause, shit's not safe, you need to stay in a public place right now...and I can't fucking deal with her anymore."

"What?"

"Nothing. Look man it's not just the cops, the other fucking gangs are still after us too."

"I need to get high."

Darren started breaking up pot for a joint, wondering what he was going to say to Sammy, and how Jessie had managed to get her to meet with him, and how long did he have until the cops get him?

+

Darren was wondering how on earth Sammy knew so much about him. Had she researched him? He was on the news after all. Maybe she was as obsessed with him as he was her. This idea made his stomach switch positions all nice. He was also wondering what she was talking about. It was hard to concentrate, with his mind racing, exhausted-nervous-drifting, and he loved watching her talk, and really-really wanted to hug/hold her, all perfect. Kisses would follow, of course. "How does a person get closer," he was wondering.

"How does a person kiss. Am I sweating cause of the cocaine?" He really wanted to reach out and take her hand, that rested all lovely on the table, right in front of *his* hand.

"Darren, I don't want you to think that I am judging you in anyway. But you're going to hell. And I don't want that to happen."

There was silence, and Darren didn't even want to ask, but he had to.

"Can I ask you a question?"

"Sure."

"Have *you* ever entered into a sex chatroom under the name Sammyman?"

Sammy's face blushed and she moment-hesitated but said, "No."

Darren made an embarrassed face, and tilted his head all lonely. He wished he hadn't asked. Sammy seemed to notice.

"Darren. It's ok. I don't think you are a freak or anything. I am really glad to meet you and I can't wait to get to know you better. O.K.? It's alright."

Sammy reached out and placed her hand on top of Darren's, all soft/sweet. And, although not wanting to seem lame, Darren couldn't help but smile-huge, all bliss-pillowy because of how happy that tiny bit of affection made him feel. This was, with out a doubt, the best, greatest, wonderfullest, slap-happy, most exciting part of Darren's whole/entire life. As she touched him; he was the most in love that he would ever be.

And then Sammy's face exploded all over Darren, and her body fell sideways out of her chair, all thump/knock, leaving Darren holding the sweet remains of her hand/arm in his.

+

Jessie knocked/rattled the basement window. Darren walked over to let him in and Jessie spoke through the window.

"Change of plans.   Meet me out front."

Darren ran upstairs and out of the front door and wondered if they were running away to another country. To get away from the cops.

`   "Well, everything is pretty much going to go down tonight or tomorrow. What's funny is that The Penetrators are positioned out all around the neighborhood, probably waiting to kill us, and the cops are all over the place too, waiting to take us in, and I don't think either side realizes the other side is there."

"Can I eat this?"

Darren found a plastic bag filled with little frozen pieces of chocolate in the car.

"Sure, give me a couple too. How long has it been since you've slept?"

"I don't know, almost a week I think. You?"

"About the same."

"Are we running away to another country? This chocolate is *really* good."

"Yeah, it's milk chocolate, crunchy peanut butter, ground up mushrooms, hash and LSD. And no we are not leaving the country. We are going to the grocery store. For snacks. We are going to make the best of this night. God dammit."

"I thought you didn't do drugs. For God."

"I think I was more not doing drugs for Sammy and the weird sex than the whole God thing. I have mixed feelings about the whole God thing right now."

Jessie and Darren thought all silently about Sammy as the drugs started seeping across them and the car bulleted for the Grocery.

+

Bullets flew all ziggazaggy past Darren, making all kinds of noise and wrecking the Quick-a-Flippers pizza. It was zip-crash-explosions all around. But he hadn't moved. He was staring at his hand, still holding the remainder of Sammy's. Back and forth from his/Sammy's hands to Sammy's corpse on the floor, silhouetted by a pool of her ever-spreading blood, wondering how she retained that angelic glow even without a face. Not really seeing any of the mayhem, not even wiping the blood dripping from his face. The restaurant was clearing out all panicky-hysteria, and Darren was wondering how on earth this stuff always happened to him? He wanted to laugh/cry or maybe bleed himself all over the place. But he did not want to move. He was paralyzed by mania-love-retardation.

A bunch of thug-kids were bending over the booths, shooting at a bunch of big Italian-mafioso-stereotype looking guys on the other side of the restaurant. Darren started watching, absentmindedly, wondering why this never happened to the kids in Saved by the Bell. He did not make an attempt to run or even duck for cover. He just stared and began to wonder if maybe he was only dreaming. Or if maybe everything was in slow motion. A thuggy kid tackled him and dragged him behind a table.

"Mother fucker, you are crazy, mother fucker thinks he's bullet proof or some shit, fuck is the matter with....."

His head exploded across Darren's face before thug-kid could even finish. Darren, with thoughts of the two separate kinds of blood and head on him, was starting to realize that the guys shooting at him and his thuggy protectors were probably the mob. He thought this mainly because they were Italian and all dressed in suits . Then he started wondering, "What is really the difference between a gang like The Penetrators and the mob, anyway?" Before he could further expound upon that thought, however, Jessie popped out from behind another booth with two hand guns, firing/killing at anything he saw. Dropping the guns, he pushed towards Darren, grabbed him, and dragged him out, staying low and using the tables for cover. He somehow managed to get Darren out to the car through the destructive, pizza-appetite/life-ending-chaos in the dining room.

"This is not fair! Fuck! I shouldn't have to deal with the fucking mafia! I'm fucking fifteen years old! They have been doing this shit their whole/entire lives!"

Jessie was crying. Probably because he had seen Sammy's body. He was screaming red-eyed and snot-face drooling.

"Its not fucking fair! I'm just a fucking kid!"

Darren had never seen him like this. So pathetic. Except for maybe in the closet, at the orphanage, but that still wasn't the same thing. And Darren had no idea why Jessie was so heartbroken.

"Its O.K. Jessie."

"No, its not! I didn't know they'd just fucking start shooting up a family restaurant! Aw, God man...why'd they have to fucking shoot her."

Jessie was all sniffle-whimpers.

"Jessie, you barely even knew Sammy. And I'll be alright, I'm used to..."

"Sammy and I were really close man."

Jessie broke down again.

"Really? But I thought you..."

"Darren...man...we've been...together for awhile..."

"What does that mean?"

"Like...having sex, man..."

Jessie had drool all over him and he was gasping for air, but Darren was calm.

"Let me out of the car. Pull over. I want to be out of this car."

"Darren we can't just stop right here...there are people after us, who want to kill..."

"STOP THE FUCKING CAR, RIGHT FUCKING NOW, YOU FUCKING ASSHOLE, FUCK YOU!"

Darren was in tears screaming.

"FUCKING LET ME OUT OF THE FUCKING CAR YOU FUCKING ASSHOLE!"

Jessie pulled over onto the side of the road even though it was dangerous, and people could very well have been after them. He did it because he had never heard Darren yell like that before. Darren got out of the car and stood there, looking at the ground. Jessie got out.

"I'm so sorry man, I didn't mean for it to happen, honestly, it happened one time and I fell for her, just like you did. I couldn't help it."

"Fuck you."

"She was strange man, and she was teaching me about God, and she was beautiful and I just fell for her. I'm sorry man."

"Fuck you. Why did you even have her meet with me then? If she was yours? You fucking asshole?"

"I didn't think I could handle her anymore. I mean she was amazing, but too guilty...too many scars...I'm sorry. I wanted her to be happy and I knew you still wanted her, so I don't know...I guess, I thought maybe you might do better than I did?"

"Fuck you..."

"Come on man, I know I fucked you over. But I just lost someone kind of special to me..."

"ME TOO! SHE WAS FUCKING SPECIAL TO ME TOO! Even if I didn't know her...I still loved her..."

The boys stood in silence for a couple minutes watching the cars drive by them. Then Darren said he wanted to go home. And Jessie told him it wasn't safe.

"Just take me home, I need my drugs...my speed is there, and I'm real tired."

"How long are you really expecting to last?"

"Till the end. Now please stop talking to me and take me home. I'm still mad at you."

+

"Oh my God, Darren. I remembered why we came into

the grocery store. Snacks. We are on a mission to get snacks."

"I'm not really hungry."

"Yes but when we smoke more pot we will get hungry."

"Yeah."

"But we have to hurry, because I remembered what we are doing tonight also."

"What?"

"I traded a guy an ounce of pot for a bunch of shitty zombie movies. That's why I came over originally."

Darren had heard of zombie movies but hadn't ever seen one.

"We are going to watch them all."

"How many movies?"

"Fifteen, I think."

"That's more than the night has time for, Jessie."

"Well, we will just watch them until the cops or the gangs come after us then."

So, after spending almost three hours in the grocery store, all sleepless and brain-egg-fried, the boys each bought a candy bar for later in the night and walked out into the parking lot to the car. They were greeted in the lot by six or seven menacing looking metal heads. A metal head is like a punk, but slighty more hilly-billy and usually bigger/fatter.

"Who are you?" Jessie asked.

"We are The Penetrators, and we're here to fuck you up."

"Really?"

"Yeah."

Jessie thought about this.

"But I thought you guys were back at his place waiting for us." He gestured towards Darren.

"No, that's not us."

"God damnit. I was hoping it was you guys. That means it's the fucking mob."

Darren started drug-giggling, for no reason other than

that it was a bad time to start laughing.

"Why would you hope it was us?"

"Well. I don't know if it's just the name, but you guys aren't really well respected in the gang world. I know you are the major speed supplier to local metal bands, and all, but no one really considers you guys a threat. "

The Metal Guys, who were probably in their thirties, drooped their heads down all hurt-sulky.

"Really? See...that's fucked up man...because...honestly...we've kind of had a complex about that shit for..."

Jessie mowed down all seven of them with dual uzies, before the Metal Head-guy could finish his sentence. "Its just a really bad name that's all. And its been a shitty couple of days." Jessie said to Darren as they got into their car. Darren still seemed shaken/scared, so Jessie continued to rationalize, "I'm sorry, but you just have to think, 'What would Wu do?' and I think that any member of the Wu Tang Clan, thrown into that situation, would have shot those guys, just like I did."

"Wait, could you explain again why we have to ask ourselves what *Wu* would do?"

"I don't know man, lets get home before this trip peaks."

+

The trip was long-flowing, watery-wet and giggle-intense-colorful. And Darren found zombie movies to be slow and silly and awesome. He envied the sense of purpose that the characters felt, when they had to constantly fight for their lives. And the strange joyfulness taken in the violent slash-killings of the docile/dumb human-shells.

The police and maybe the mafia, or maybe the FBI or DEA were outside. But the sleepiness made the boys forget. They ate their candy bars and watched movie after movie, tripping so hard, they forgot that they needed to keep doing other drugs in order to stay awake.

They kept going though. After the first couple, they found that not all of the movies were zombie movies. Some were vampire movies and one was about werewolves. But the story premise was usually the same, with just a different kind of makeup applied to the bad guys. They smoked a joint at sunrise and wondered if maybe the police weren't going to ever raid the place. They popped another zombie movie in called, "Zombie," and wondered if maybe all the gang members arrested were loyal and hadn't snitched after all. Or maybe the cops weren't allowed to move in on them, because Yuppie-Parents were so rich/powerful.

This thought comforted them as they came down. And their brains started to enjoy this strange relaxing-quiet feeling. So warm and clear that they both forgot to stay awake and to worry about everything. Darren forgot his drugs and Jessie forgot to repent. They had one last, tired-conversation together and then fell asleep.

+

Now, one might think that after not sleeping for a week, my brain would be content just shutting down. That it would be happy to not think of anything for hours. But if it really is our big fleshy-brains that somehow spawn our dreams and spin ideas, that flip my sleeping body all over this world; then my brain did not shut down that night.

I dreamed that I woke up in a zombie dimension. It was the same world, but I just knew that zombies were all over the place and that I needed to beware and I realized that I didn't have a weapon and that I would need a bat or something, and then I remembered Yuppie-Dad's vault, and I wasted no time unlocking it. I started loading gun after gun, sticking as many guns and knives as I could into my belt. It was urgent, I didn't have any time, like all the zombies were probably already in the house, or at least surrounding the place. And I hear a window break and then another one and I am flustered, loading every gun I can reach. And the light in the vault goes out, but there is a little bit of moonlight, and I see something crawling into the window, and I aim the gatling gun towards the general area of the window and a whirl of fire-noise explodes out of the end and now there is twice as big of a hole where the window used to be, and I'm cursing myself for making their entrance-way even more convenient. Two zombies stumbling down the stairs and they start running towards me and I can tell that it's the Yuppie-Parents, but they have a blood lust in their eyes that I haven't seen before and I know that they are undead and unload a sawed off shot gun at the last second, taking their heads off and they are pouring in through the windows now, Jessie is by my side with an assault rifle shooting the zombies as they come in, yelling, "Fuck you guys! Fuck you all!" And one grabs my ankle and I shoot him or her in the face and see that a big one is on top of Jessie and he is screaming and another one jumps on the pile and Jessie is yelling for me, dead-already, bitten and I know that I can't let him be eaten alive. So, I toss three grenades into the vault, saying, "I'm sorry." And I'm running out of the vault, diving away and the explosion is massive, and Jessie is dead. And something is on top of me so I stick a knife up through the bottom of his chin and roll him off of me, all blood. And I'm shooting and throwing grenades out of a window hoping to try and scare the zombies away from this house. And Jessie is dead, and I'm wondering if there was something I could have done, running out of the house that's caught fire from the grenades and I see cars lined up outside and it is the police, and I am thinking that they must think I am a zombie because they are shooting at me, and I see Bob running towards me in his robe and underwear, yelling to the cops, telling them that I am not a zombie, but the cops keep shooting at me, and I'm scared/yelling that they are going to hit Bob, so I start shooting this machine gun at them, I forget what kind it was, but it was huge and I lost control of it and accidentally shot Bob's legs out from underneath him. And so I dropped it, all screaming, and ran over to him saying sorry-sorry-sorry, what was he doing there, but the cops were still trying to shoot at me, I think, because, when he lifted his head to look at me all painful eyes, it blew up all over me. That's when I woke up. Bullets flying by, Yuppie-House in flames behind me, Bob dead on the ground next to me, dead all over me. I'm starting to understand what was happening in my dream-world and what was happening in this one, when I am tackled by the swat-team on the front lawn and they put my hands on my head. How could I be so stupid? And I'm knowing, right then and there, that there will be no explaining this.

Darren, on the couch and Jessie on the floor, their bodies were shutting down.

"Since you just found God and then kind of lost him again, what do you think happens now--after we die?"

Jessie spoke all slurred slow, almost asleep, eyes closed.

"I sometimes think that all of our mind-worries vanish. And our force of life frees itself from our meat-prisons and spreads itself out amongst the whole world of energy, and we flow, without thinking, only *feeling* the throbbing ever building pulsation of bliss/unity. But then, honestly, I can't really truly believe anything for more than five minutes at a time."

+

Darren slept and cried in his jail cell. Waiting for a trial. Knowing that no one would believe him. Knowing he would go down in history as the mastermind of a notorious child-gang, a heartless murderer, and a drug addict. All evil. But he didn't really care. His tears were for the Yuppie-Parents and they were for Bob and they were for Jessie. And they were partially for himself too. And they were for his Hippie-Parents and they were for Sammyman.

The guards said that Darren's moans did not stop at night. In fact, those first couple days, when he slept, his moans apparently evolved into screams. This was because he was going through drug withdrawl and this was because he was all alone and this was because of his Dad and this was because of his Mom. When he wasn't crying, he would write down some of his story, in the first person style that Jessie had suggested.

Lawyers were trying to attatch themselves to Darren again. Visiting him in his jail cell. He just let them talk, knowing that they were wasting their breath. He didn't want a trial. He did not want to explain, that all of these things he had done, all of his actions, all of the mayhem. It had come from somewhere else, or something else that he just wouldn't ever understand. He didn't want to tell people this, because they would all want to know the exact same thing, he'd always wanted to know: "What's controlling me when I'm not?" He would never find out the answer to this question. And he would never have a trial.

The night before his day in court, after falling asleep, he crept out of bed all puppet-like, dreaming/sleepwalking one last time. He sat at a desk, pulled out a sheet of paper and wrote the last little section of this book, just the same way he'd written the majority of it. Asleep.

Then he scooted the chair a couple of inches away from the desk and slowly/carefully leaned his head back. He tensed up his neck and slammed his face down-hard onto the edge of the table, at just the right angle and with enough force-precision to drive the bones in his nose way up through his brain. He was all dead, instantly.

About the Author

Brian j. Kamerer is a true blue rags to riches story, an up and coming, totally hyped up author, whose literature is changing the face of reading and writing in America and all over the world. He has been praised and acclaimed by rich *and* famous people alike, and Ernest Hemingway once had this to say about him, "He does what I do, even better than how I did it." Brian plays piano and sings in a band called *JoesFriendBrian* and plays drums for a band called *Black Mold*. He has many books in the works and he is also an accomplished film actor, writer and director. He also belongs to a cult type thing called The Wrong Man. To see movies and hear music and learn more about Brian or The Wrong Man go to www.wrongmanproductions.com

CPSIA information can be obtained at www.ICGtesting.com
Printed in the USA
LVOW07s1617140216

474949LV00002BA/142/P